DREAM HUNTER

THE BAILEY SPADE SERIES: BOOK 2

DIMA ZALES

♠ MOZAIKA PUBLICATIONS ♠

Copyright © 2021 Dima Zales and Anna Zaires
www.dimazales.com

Published by Mozaika Publications, an imprint of Mozaika LLC.
www.mozaikallc.com

Cover by Orina Kafe
www.orinakafe.design

e-ISBN: 978-1-63142-613-1
Print ISBN: 978-1-63142-614-8

CHAPTER ONE

I STAND on the surface of a calm black ocean, with fiery, angry-looking skies above my head. Six humanoid figures are sprinting toward me, their strange feet making them look like they're tiptoeing on the water. Their right index fingers sport sword-like claws, and they lack noses and eyes. In general, their heads are pretty lacking—no hair, no ears, just baby-smooth skin and a huge mouth in the middle of where the face would be. And if that weren't creepy enough, the horror nearest me starts screeching like a cat in heat.

To my shock, I realize it's saying something.

"You!" the creature is shrieking. "You're not dead?"

I gape at it. "Why would I be? What are you? How do you know me?"

The creature slices at me with its sword-claw, and I duck to avoid losing my head.

"Stay still!" the monstrosity screeches. "If I slay you now, Master will be pleased."

Yeah, right. An appendage-like growth extends from my wrist, turning into a furry sword in time to parry the next sword-claw strike. "What master?" I demand as I lunge and slash.

My opponent's cleaved in half before it can answer.

A second creature reaches me, swinging its sword-claw. "Master hates you!" it screeches when I parry. "Your existence is a blight."

I counterattack with my furry blade, burying it in my opponent's chest. "Me, a blight?" I yank out the blade. "Talk about the pot calling the kettle black."

The time for talking about their master must be over. The next two attackers come at me with even greater violence. Their claws hack and slash without any strategy, making them easy prey for my furry blade.

The next two are more cautious. They circle me silently, looking for an opening.

I feint, then lop one's head right off. The next opponent ducks beneath my blade by crouching on the water. As I loom over it, it strikes out with its claw, stabbing me in the thigh.

I jump back, crying out in pain. The affected muscle burns agonizingly.

The monster goes for the kill, but I parry. With a screeching yell, it lunges again—and its claw pierces my shoulder.

Ignoring the dizzying wave of agony, I swing my blade and slice its head clean off.

———

I'M in a huge palatial lobby with reddish green walls and yellowish blue marble floors, the richly appetizing scent of manna filling my nostrils as impossibly shaped objects float in front of my eyes.

My dream palace. I made it.

Blood is still oozing from my thigh and shoulder. Pucking puck. That subdream was worse than others. If there'd been one more monster in there, I'd be foaming at the mouth and trying to kill everyone in the waking world. It's a good thing I asked Mom's doctor to prepare for that eventuality. If I'd emerged from my dreamwalking trance in a homicidal mood, he could've subdued me with the help of the burly security guys he brought in—or knocked me out with whatever's in his syringe.

Well, the good thing is, none of that is necessary now, since I'm safely in the dream world. I exit my body, heal it, give myself a fiery hair makeover, and jump back into myself.

Pom shows up next to one of the impossible shapes. He's a looft, a symbiotic creature permanently attached to my wrist who's also my companion here in the dream world. The size of a large bird, with gargantuan lavender-colored eyes, triangular pointy ears, and fluffy fur that changes colors to match his emotions, he usually belongs in the dictionary next to the word "cute."

Currently, though, he's solid black and his ears are droopy. "I accidentally read your mind again," he confesses guiltily. "You're here to wake up Lidia, aren't you?"

Reminded of my important mission, I take flight, heading for the tower of sleepers. "That's right. Mom was stuck in non-REM sleep—hence the subdream we just experienced."

He zooms around me, shuddering. "Scary."

"For sure. But hey, you were a sword this time." I demonstrate by recreating the weapon I just used. "Did you have any clue that was actually a dream?"

He turns an even darker black. "No. I was just living in the moment, not questioning being that sword—as weird as that sounds."

"Same here. No clue I was dreaming."

Pom circles around my head. "The creatures spoke this time."

So they did. How weird. I think back to all the other subdreams I've experienced and the bizarre, terrifying creatures I've met in them. "Maybe they've always tried to speak," I say. "But this time, they had mouths that let them be understood."

Pom's fur takes on a light orange hue. "Where do subdreams come from?"

I slow my flight. He's raised a question I've pondered a lot, without ever coming up with a satisfactory answer. "I don't know. I've nicknamed them subdreams because I think they tap deeper into the subconscious than regular dreams do."

"Whose subconscious, yours or the dreamer's?"

"Great question." I conjure up the creatures from the subdream I experienced when I invaded Bernard's non-REM sleep—the ones that look like oversized bacteria and viruses. "Theoretically, these could be my fears of contamination made flesh."

Pom peers at them as I recreate the creatures I encountered in Gertrude's subdream—tentacled giant naked mole rats riding warthog-spider hybrids. "Nothing about these riders fits that pattern," I say, studying them, "so they might be something Gertrude dreamed up."

Pom floats in front of my face. "So you think it was your mom who created the monsters we just defeated?"

"Could be. Though I don't like the implications."

He blinks at me.

"The monsters said their master hated me," I explain. "If Mom created them, she'd be their master, right?" Reaching the glass-walled tower of sleepers, I locate the nook where Mom's form resides now that I've forced her into REM sleep. "I know we had that fight before her accident," I continue as I fly toward it, "but I hope she doesn't *really* feel that my existence is a blight—whatever that means."

Pom flies next to me. "You feel bad about that fight, don't you?"

"Of course. I made Mom think I might invade her dreams, something she made me promise never to do.

That's why she got so upset and stormed out. Her accident wouldn't have happened if it weren't for my big mouth."

Pom turns gray, a color rare for him. "You didn't know what would happen."

"True." I take a breath to suppress the heavy swell of emotions thinking about Mom's accident always generates. "In any case, it doesn't matter now. I *am* breaking my promise."

"To save her life."

"Yes." Outside, in the waking world, Mom is in a strange coma-like sleep, one that neither Isis, a powerful healer, nor Dr. Xipil, a rare gnome doctor, could get her out of. The only thing left to try was for me to go into her dreams and wake her from within.

Hopefully she'll understand and forgive me.

Entering her nook, I land next to the bed. To my surprise, there's no trauma loop cloud above her head —something I always suspected I'd find if I dreamwalked in her. Before the accident, she'd displayed all the symptoms I've seen in my most troubled clients.

"I'm sure she'll forgive you," Pom says sagely, landing behind me. "What's more important is that you forgive yourself. From my experience, that's harder."

I turn to see if he's kidding, but he's still that depressing gray color. "What experience are you talking about? What did you ever need to forgive yourself for?"

His cute face twists into a miserable expression, and

his ears droop. "I permanently attached myself to you without asking your permission."

So he had. I certainly hadn't expected to end up with a symbiont when I petted a mooft—a cow-like creature loofts normally live on—at a Gomorran zoo. But now I can't imagine my life without him.

"Sweetie." I snatch him up, bringing him up to my eye level. "I already told you, I wouldn't want to take you off even if I could."

The tips of his ears turn a light shade of purple. "You told me that when you thought you'd be executed. Now that you know you'll live, do you still mean it?"

"We're symbionts for life," I say solemnly. "Don't you ever forget it."

The rest of Pom turns purple, and he grins. "We make a good pair of symbionts, don't we?"

"I don't know what I'd do without you." I kiss his furry forehead and set him down. "Now how about I do what I came here to do?"

We both look over at Mom. Her beautiful features appear so peaceful in her slumber.

"Do you want some privacy?" Pom asks.

"Please." It's been four months since Mom entered her coma. The chances that I'll cry when we finally speak are pretty high, and seeing that might upset Pom.

He obligingly disappears.

I place my hand on Mom's forehead. "I'm sorry," I whisper. "If I could save you without breaking my promise, I would."

Steeling myself, I dive into her dream.

7

CHAPTER TWO

MOM IS CHOPPING something in an unfamiliar kitchen, while a child version of me is opening a packet of manna.

My younger self looks to be about five and must be filtered through Mom's memories. I doubt I was *that* adorable, and I'm skeptical of that innocence in my eyes. Though I don't remember anything from when I was younger than seven, I couldn't have changed *this* much.

A part of me is disappointed. My dreamwalker powers allow me to tell if a dream is based on a memory, and that's not the case here. It would've been a chance to learn something of my early years—one of Mom's many taboo subjects.

Mom starts chopping with greater intensity.

Something prevents me from clearing my throat to inform her of my presence. As much as I yearn to speak with her, curiosity and a certain intuition lead me to observe for now. I turn invisible—and just in time.

Clutching the knife so hard her knuckles turn white, Mom lunges at the little me.

What the puck?

Mom's face is an unrecognizable mask of hatred as she stabs the little me in the heart. My child self screams in pain—which is the only thing that covers my shocked gasp.

I disable my sounds and breathe deeply to calm myself.

It's just a dream. Dreams can be chaotic and crazy. This doesn't mean Mom wants to kill me.

What I just saw doesn't have to be a manifestation of Mom's anger about our fight.

A new dream starts.

We're in our apartment on Gomorrah. Mom is watching as a teenage version of me stands in the middle of the room with a VR headset on her head. As I look around, I notice something curious—some of the windows around us are black.

I first came across the concept of a black window in the notes of Leal, the murdered dreamwalker from the New York Council, and I learned more about them in the dreams of Nina, the telekinetic who acted as a sort of memory storage for said dreamwalker. Nina herself had a troublesome memory that she'd had Leal lock away behind a black window.

Is that the case for Mom? Are these windows events that she, or someone else, erased from memory? It could explain why she didn't have a trauma loop. Whatever's troubling her could be hidden behind the black windows.

Before I can follow this chain of thought further, the same look of hatred appears on Mom's face, and she tackles the unaware teenage me like an NFL linebacker, shoving her with all her might.

My teenage self flies at one of the regular windows. Flailing, she crashes through the glass and plummets to the pavement far below.

What. The. Hell?

The dream changes again. This version of me looks to be ten or so, and is sleeping. Mom is looming over her with that same frightening expression on her face.

"Please tell me you just want to dreamwalk in her," I whisper, but she can't hear me. My voice is still disabled.

Grabbing a pillow, Mom places it over the face of the sleeping me, smothering her.

Puck.

I give myself the ability to make sounds again and become visible.

"Mom," I say tightly. "I think you're stuck in some hellish nightmare."

At least I hope that's what's happening. There's no way she's enjoying killing me over and over like that. I wasn't *that* annoying of a daughter.

Confusion replaces hatred on Mom's face.

"You're dreaming," I say quickly. "This—"

"You're dreamwalking in me!" Mom looks furious enough to kill the real version of me this time.

I instinctively back away. "You don't understand. I didn't have a choice."

She points her hand at me, and an arc of lightning shoots from her fingers into my head.

I feel like someone's turned me into a lemon, squeezed me dry, and blended the leftover meat and peel into a smoothie.

I open my mouth to scream, but it's too late.

I'm no longer in the dream world.

CHAPTER THREE

I'M BACK in the hospital room, with Dr. Xipil and the burly security guys watching me intently, ready to subdue me in case I became a psychotic killer.

I paste a smile on my lips, even though I'm freaking out. The last thing I need is for Dr. Xipil to stab me with that syringe he's holding.

"What happened?" he asks with a worried expression.

"It didn't work," I say and place my hand back on Mom's forehead. It's strangely clammy. "I'm going to try again."

"Wait—"

Tuning out the gnome doctor's objections, I will myself to return into Mom's dreams.

Nothing happens.

Huh.

I touch my furry wristband—Pom—trying to get into the dream world that way.

Nothing. There's no scent of ozone, no sensation of falling that comes along with the transition into a dreamwalking trance. I might as well be touching a rock.

I grip Mom's hand and strain harder. Still nothing. Eventually, I have to accept it: The violent dream world expulsion Mom performed on me robbed me of my powers for the day.

Unbelievable.

I didn't realize such a thing was possible—or that Mom could do it. In general, her dreamwalking powers seem to be much stronger than mine.

What's extra amazing is that Mom is this strong despite having lived here on Gomorrah for as long as I can remember. Us Cognizant slowly lose our powers unless we regularly travel to Otherlands that contain humans, like Earth.

Dr. Xipil exchanges a glance with the guard nearest me. "Are you sure you're okay?"

Puck. He's worried I *am* homicidal.

I force another smile to my lips. "I'm fine. I'm just disappointed I failed."

"As I was trying to tell you, you didn't *just* fail." The doctor nods at the screens monitoring Mom's heartbeat and brain activity. "Your dreamwalking drove her vitals through the roof."

"What?" I peer at the monitors, wishing I had medical training. I know a lot about sleep, but not much else. "How?"

"I don't know, but she had a dangerously fast

heartbeat, shortness of breath, excessive sweating and trembling—all signs of a nocturnal panic attack, but without the awakening that typically follows."

My stomach sinks as I look Mom over. Her forehead is beaded with sweat, and her bronzed skin has a gray tinge. "So what do I do?"

Dr. Xipil adjusts his breathing mask, an apparatus all gnomes wear due to their anatomy. "Well… it's a unique case. Your powers may still be the best way to wake her, but you might want to let her body recover for a day or two before you try anything else."

I take a deep breath. "Actually, I don't know if it's worth trying again." I explain my theory that Mom may be much more powerful than I am.

He gestures for the security guys to leave. "Maybe you can reason with her next time?"

"I told you, she doesn't want me dreamwalking in her." I look at Mom, my chest squeezing with guilt at the ashen hue of her face. "Maybe I should've listened."

Dr. Xipil readjusts his mask. "I'll see what we can do on our end. Meanwhile, we have to reattach some life support."

On my wrist, Pom turns black—reflecting my emotions this time. I swallow against the bitter lump in my throat. "I understand."

"You might also want to talk to a sleep expert," the doctor says. "Or find another dreamwalker."

I blink at him. "I don't know another dreamwalker." We're not exactly thick on the ground.

He regards me speculatively. "In that case, have you ever heard of Dr. Cipactli?"

I shake my head.

"He's a sleep expert with a great reputation. He heads up the ZIZZ Sleep Clinic." Dr. Xipil's chin lifts. "Not surprising, really, as he's a fellow gnome."

I'm genuinely impressed. "Yet another gnome in a medical field?"

Dr. Xipil huffs through his mask. "I was as surprised as you. I know I'm an outlier. I became a doctor when I lost my parents to a rare genetic disease. Still, even I can't fathom why a fellow gnome would want to study sleep of all things."

He can say that again. Gnomes usually thrive in technology-heavy fields. My friend Itzel, for instance, is obsessed with space exploration and gadgets of all kinds, and her famous grandfather, Cadmael, invented the Vega reactors that run everything on Gomorrah.

"I'll talk to this Dr. Cipactli," I say.

"Great." Dr. Xipil makes some gestures in the air. "I just sent you his info."

"Thank you. Can you also give it to me verbally? My comms died, and I haven't replaced them." Actually, my comms were crushed by a vampire on Earth—but who's keeping track.

Dr. Xipil tells me where I need to go and adds, "I'll talk to Dr. Cipactli right after I leave, and send him all the information about your mother."

I thank him again, and he leaves the room. I clasp

Mom's hand again. "Bye," I tell her softly. "I'll see you soon, okay?"

There's no reply. With a heavy heart, I head out.

———

AS I WALK past the nurses in the hallway, I ponder why Mom kept killing me in her dream. The best answer I can come up with is that even though I was invisible, she'd detected my dreamwalking presence and it'd angered her. After all, my whole life I'd promised her I *wouldn't* enter her dreams.

But why was she killing me at different ages? Why not just push me out the way she did when I made my presence known?

More importantly, should I respect her wishes and not go back?

I try to imagine leaving her hooked up on those machines indefinitely, and everything inside me revolts at the thought. Even if I can come up with the money to keep her in the paid hospital long term, she'll eventually waste away, machines or not. If I don't wake her, she's as good as dead.

So that's that. Unless the sleep expert can come up with another solution, I'm going to have to figure out a way to gain more power, go back, and try waking her up again. I even have an idea when it comes to power gathering—

The hospital doors slide open, and I look around.

This is the Health District, named so due to the

slew of paid hospitals, pharmaceutical companies, and research centers all around. It vaguely resembles Gardens by the Bay in Singapore, as the water-collecting trees here look a lot like the Supertrees there.

My destination is walkable, so I make my way through the busy crowds of fellow Cognizant. After Earth, seeing so many non-humanoid pedestrians is a little jarring, especially when I spot a couple of weres in their animal shapes.

The building where the sleep clinic resides is small and reminds me of the Freedom Tower in New York. I go inside and take the elevator to the sleep clinic floor. An elf secretary tells me the soonest I can see Dr. Cipactli is tomorrow afternoon, no matter how urgent my issue is.

Cursing under my breath at the delay, I leave the building and locate the nearest store where I can buy a replacement comms device; without it, I feel like a cavewoman.

"Would you like to check out the newest model?" the uber saleswoman asks me with a megawatt smile.

I look around. "Is there a place I can check my cc balance?"

She nods at a nearby mirror, and I realize it's a screen in disguise.

I walk up to the screen, authenticate myself, and have a look at my money.

Wait a second. The number here is much bigger than I expected.

It doesn't take long for me to figure out what happened. Valerian paid nearly double the amount we agreed upon. Wow. He's given me bonuses for a job well done before, but never this much.

Once I have my comms, I'll need to thank him. With this amount, I can pay Mom's outstanding bills and still have enough left over to consider the newest, most expensive model of comms.

"Show me," I say to the uber woman.

She takes out a sleek-looking comms device I've never seen before and opens it like a clam shell—another novelty.

Inside the comms are almost invisible earphones, two contact lenses, and ten clip-on nails.

I examine it all in awe. "I've heard these were in development, but didn't realize they were out."

My last set of comms interfaced via special glasses and gloves, so I couldn't openly use them on Earth. This is so much stealthier.

"Put them on," she says with a knowing grin.

I reach for the contact lenses, then yank my hand back. "Are these new?"

She cocks her head. "Are you from some Otherland?" Before I can tell her I'm local, she adds, "These comms have *hygieia* built in—a cleaning technology."

I know what she's talking about, of course. Hygieia is why things like salmonella are extinct on Gomorrah. Her answer also tells me the stuff *was* in other people's eyes before—which is a problem, even though I know my concern is not rational. It's like drinking out of a sterilized toilet on Earth—icky, at least to me.

She must read my mind because she smiles sagely and takes out a sealed unit.

"I don't promise to buy it," I say reluctantly.

"That's fine." She hands it to me.

Right. She knows the next customer won't have my qualms.

I unwrap the device as if it were a Christmas gift, put in the contacts, and whistle under my breath. They're extremely comfortable—as in, I don't feel them at all.

The saleswoman smiles wider. She knows I'm almost on the hook.

The earphones are amazing. Once in my ears, it's impossible to see them, and I can still hear external sounds.

I hold the nail things to my nails, and they latch on as if magnetized. The result isn't bad at all—a bit like if I got blue gel nails on Earth.

"Are the gestures the same as with the gloves?" I ask.

She nods, so I gesture for the comms to activate.

The usual spherical icons appear in the air in front of me. With glasses, these looked like *Star Wars* holograms, but the contacts make everything sharper, almost real.

I gesture at the login app, and once I'm in, the interface changes to the way I'd previously set it up, with icons that look like impossible shapes, such as the

Penrose triangle. It gives me the feeling that I'm in the dream world.

I have a ton of messages waiting, but before I check them, I bring up the paying app and say, "I'll take this."

"Pleasure doing business with you." The saleswoman grins her widest smile yet.

As I walk out, I check some of my messages. Most are from the hospital, telling me I must pay the bills. I do that and then craft a message to Valerian. He's instrumental to my new idea on how to gather more power—at least that's what I tell myself.

This has nothing to do with what almost happened between us the other day.

Nothing at all.

To my disappointment, he doesn't instantly reply. Nor does he reply by the time I get into a car. Well, he does spend half his time on Earth and half on Gomorrah, so hopefully he's just away and not ignoring me.

The car drops me off by our building, a modest skyscraper with one hundred and fifty floors.

Stepping into the apartment is an odd experience after being away. The first thing that stands out, as usual, is how few personal touches Mom gave the place. The walls are bare, and the kitchen is immaculately clean. There are showrooms at furniture stores with more personality. If I were to enter Mom's bedroom, it would be even more bland—just walls and a bed. Sometimes I wonder if Mom thought that by decorating, she might accidentally reveal to me some secret from her past.

I enter my own room. Like inside my virtual reality interface—and dream world—I have a lot of art that features visual paradoxes and surreal scenarios. Works reminiscent of Earth's M. C. Escher and Salvador Dalí slideshow on screens that are my room's walls. On the ancient portable screen that I borrowed from Mom, I spot the cover of the textbook on video game design I was reading before my life turned upside down. My unmade bed is floating a couple of inches off the ground thanks to magnets and superconductivity, and it looks ridiculously inviting.

I guess those four months without sleep are still weighing on me.

Yawning, I check to see if Valerian has replied.

He hasn't.

I guess I might as well use the wait time to chip away at my sleep debt.

I program my comms to ring loudly if I get a message, and I set an alarm so I don't miss my appointment with Dr. Cipactli. I doubt I'll need the latter—it would mean I'd slept over twenty hours. Still, better safe than sorry.

Picking up a hygieia wand, I properly disinfect myself and plop onto the bed. Immediately, my tense muscles relax. Earth's best memory foam mattresses are a joke compared to smart beds on Gomorrah. I feel like I've been enveloped in a cloud, with the floating sensation completing that illusion.

Not surprisingly, I go under faster than if I'd inhaled sleeping gas.

———

I WAKE to the blaring of an alarm.

Puck. I slept all the way into the next day, and now I need to rush to see Dr. Cipactli.

I gleefully use my highly sanitary, eco-friendly bathroom. My least favorite part of Earth is all that filthy water wasted as part of the plumbing. The only water we have on Gomorrah is the drinking kind coming out of the faucets, and I imbibe it with gusto. Next, I hygieia my body and teeth, put on a nondescript black shirt and dark cargo pants—one of my many outfits calibrated to fit both Earth and Gomorrah fashions—and rush out of the building. Once on the street, I get some manna and jump into a self-driving car.

Munching on the yumminess, I realize I didn't have a single dream in over twenty hours of sleep. In general, I feel great. Way better than before I slept— which tells me I needed the whole twenty hours, if not more.

The car stops, and I go up to Dr. Cipactli's office.

"I have an appointment," I tell the elf secretary.

With a polite smile, she presses some button only she can see in her VR. "One moment."

A few seconds later, the tallest gnome I've ever seen steps out of the nearby office. Gnomes grow tall in adolescence and then shrink as they grow older, so this specimen must be young—which can still mean up to a thousand years old given the typical gnome lifespan.

Like most other gnomes, this one needs to wear a special mask due to the respiratory problems they develop on worlds with air that's about twenty percent oxygen—like Earth and Gomorrah. According to Itzel, these breathing issues are what initially drove gnomes to explore technology.

Dr. Cipactli's mask is unusual in that you can't really see much of his face under its shiny black surface. If Felix were here, I bet he'd say this mask makes Dr. Cipactli look like Darth Vader.

"Bailey," he says in a deep voice distorted by the mask—strengthening the Vader comparison. "It's a pleasure to meet you." He extends his hand in an Earth-like greeting.

Ignoring the proffered appendage, I curtsy—which usually lets me avoid skin-to-skin contact.

It works. Dr. Cipactli inclines his head and says, "Step into my office."

I follow him in and do a double take.

His wall screens slideshow horror-movie-worthy images that remind me of the creatures I've met in subdreams.

"I study nightmares," he explains, noticing my shock. "Which is why I got excited when Dr. Xipil told me about your case."

I take a seat in a hovering chair and cross my legs. "Oh?"

He examines me as if I were a celebrity—or an exotic bug. "I've never met a dreamwalker before."

I smile uncomfortably. "We are pretty rare."

"Exceedingly." He sits behind his desk. "Which is why, in lieu of payment, I hope you'll demonstrate your powers."

Payment, right. This isn't a free hospital, either. I uncross my legs. "I'd be happy to. The only issue is that you're a gnome. You're not the first one to ask this of me, and I'll tell you the same thing I told them: It may or may not work."

Gnomes are renowned for being immune to many Cognizant powers. Vampire glamour doesn't work on them, tricksters can't influence their fate directly, illusionists fail to make them see their illusions, seers can't see them in their visions of the future—the list goes on and on.

Dr. Cipactli nods eagerly. "Gnome resistance to dreamwalking is why I want to try this. My grandmother told me it would work if a gnome gave consent—but didn't explain further. Once I grew up, I realized what she said doesn't make sense. If I'm sleeping—and therefore unconscious—how can I give my consent?"

Hmm. Interesting. "Maybe you agree I dreamwalk in you while you're awake?"

"Maybe." He rubs the chin part of his mask. "But wouldn't that give you unlimited dream access forever and ever? Or can I revoke my consent after I wake up?

Or maybe even during the dreamwalking session itself?"

I smile. "Now I'm actually curious to do this."

"Excellent." He leaps to his feet. "How about we try it right now?"

"One second." I turn away from him and use Pom to go in and out of the dream world.

Good. My powers have recovered.

I turn back to him. "Now's fine. Do you have a place to sleep?"

"This is a sleep clinic," he says and strides to the door.

I follow him through a corridor and into a large hall brimming with floating beds. On each bed is a sleeper. Some have IV bags attached to them, some don't. Many are also strapped to their beds, like dangerous madmen.

What the puck?

Then I recognize one of them, and things become clearer.

It's Gertrude, the New York Councilor who hates my guts. She suffers from a condition that sounds like REM Sleep Behavior Disorder—which combines poorly with her ability to give gangrene to anyone she touches. That must be what's going on with the other tied-up patients as well: They have some dangerous sleep disorders.

In any case, I'm glad Gertrude found this clinic. I recently learned that she killed someone she cared about in her sleep, so it would be good if she got the help she needs. I just hope she doesn't wake up and see me; not only does she hate me for not being able to solve her problem with my dreamwalking, but I knocked her unconscious the other day, and she might hold a grudge.

"How about here?" Dr. Cipactli points at an empty bed.

I cast a wary glance at Gertrude. "I'd prefer to do it someplace more private."

Nodding in understanding, the gnome leads me to an empty room with a bed and medical equipment that reminds me of Mom's setup.

"Would this work?" he asks.

"Sure. Are you going to be able to sleep on demand, or do you have sleeping gas on hand?"

"Something even better." He takes out a small gizmo. "A drug developed for my research. Puts the subject right into REM sleep."

Huh. Sounds like the drug Leal, the dreamwalker from the New York Council, developed. Of course, Leal's drug had an itsy-bitsy side-effect: whoever took it never woke up again. I assume Dr. Cipactli's drug isn't like that; otherwise, I'm about to partake in the strangest form of assisted suicide in history.

"I'll need to remove my mask to use this," he says gravely. There's a strange look in his eyes— embarrassment, maybe? "Will you please put it back on my face?"

I nod vigorously.

The gnome lies down and slides off his mask.

Poor guy. I now see why he wears a mask that covers so much. He must've been in an accident or something; the right side of his face is twisted by scars that look like a chemical burn.

He points the gizmo at his face and activates it.

There's a distinct hiss.

The medicine is odorless and seems to take effect immediately. His eyes start to move rapidly behind their lids.

I hygieia his mask on both sides and put it back on him. Then I hygieia his exposed forearm and place my fingers on it.

Here we go. I'm about to dreamwalk in a gnome.

CHAPTER FOUR

EXCEPT NOTHING HAPPENS when I will myself to go in.

Wait, no. Something *is* happening. Something odd.

The more I strain my powers, the more I get the feeling that I have a small voice in my head. It reminds me of how Pom communicates with me when he's awake; only it doesn't sound like my furry friend.

The voice seems to be saying, *Who are you, and what do you want?*

Feeling silly, I do what I'd do if it were Pom. Mentally, I reply, *I'm Bailey. You asked me to visit your dreams.*

No mental reply comes; instead, something yields, and with a whiff of ozone, I plummet into the gnome's dream world.

AS SOON AS I show up in my dream palace, I teleport to the tower of sleepers.

"How did it go with Lidia?" Pom's voice inquires. Then he appears bit by bit, in a Cheshire cat fashion.

"Not great," I say and bring him up to speed on what happened.

He glances at a nook nearby. "And that's the gnome doctor?"

"That's him." I fly to my target, with Pom next to me.

As soon as he notices the scar on Dr. Cipactli's face, his ears turn black. "I'm going to stay out."

"Fair enough." I touch the gnome's forearm and will myself to go in.

This time, there's no voice in my head. I simply fall into the gnome's dream.

———

FOR A MOMENT, I think I accidentally woke up.

We're back in the exact same room where Dr. Cipactli went to sleep.

Of course, if it were the waking world, there wouldn't be two of me here. The second me is wearing a cruel expression and holding Dr. Cipactli's neck in a death grip.

"You leave me no choice," the gnome croaks out, forming a ball of lightning with his hands.

Boom.

Her chest a charred mess, the second me smashes into a wall and slides down, dead.

Hey now. Why is everyone dreaming about killing me?

The dream world changes again.

Maskless and without his scar, a younger Dr. Cipactli is standing next to a ginormous machine made up of steam engines, levers, and pistons indicative of technology even more primitive than that of Earth.

An older gnome shoots a section of the device with a lightning ball—powering devices is how gnomes usually use that ability of theirs.

"The number values will be represented by gear wheels," the elder says as the ball flies at its target. "Each digit of a number has its own—"

As the ball lands, something explodes.

"Oh, no!" the elder gnome shouts.

A hissing liquid splashes Dr. Cipactli in the face.

As he screams, I realize this nightmare is a memory. This is how he got hurt.

The dream changes yet again.

This time, Dr. Cipactli is his current age, but still without the mask and scar. Nightmarish creatures that look like the images in his office appear all around us. This isn't a memory, at all.

"This is enough." I turn the nightmare beings into fluffy kittens. "You wanted a demonstration of my power, so here it is."

Dr. Cipactli gapes at me, openmouthed.

"This is a dream." I turn the kittens into tiger cubs to illustrate my point.

He rubs his eyes. "I can't believe it."

"Don't you remember giving me consent to go into your dreams? I heard you ask me who I was and what I wanted."

"I asked what?" He shakes his head. "This is so much stranger than I thought."

"Yeah." I take us to my cloud office and gesture for him to sit where my clients usually would. "Now, about my mom."

"Right." He sits and assumes his usual professional demeanor. "I reviewed all the records and concur that she needs to be awakened from inside her dreams."

I plop into my own chair. "As in, by me?"

"Not necessarily." Probably without realizing it, he makes his scar reappear on his face, followed by the mask. "We can use the same medicine on her as I used on myself."

I sit up straighter. "The one that puts you into REM sleep?"

"Right. What I forgot to tell you is that it does more than that." He pauses. "As you noticed, I had nightmares. That's not a coincidence. The medication —Koshmar—is very consistent in eliciting that response."

"Your drug gives its users nightmares?" I make my hair fiery.

His eyes widen, but he quickly composes himself and nods. "Koshmar was specifically formulated for that purpose, so it's much more potent than a drug that merely has that as a side effect. It's invaluable to my research."

I frown. "You want to give my mom a potent nightmare?"

"Yes," he says eagerly. "Koshmar nightmares get progressively worse until the sleeper wakes up, which is what we want in this case. Furthermore, an interesting aspect of these specific nightmares is that the first one always features whatever the sleeper experienced last—in your mom's case, a bad car crash. I bet she'd wake up just from that."

I regard him thoughtfully. "So this is why your first nightmare was set in the room where you fell asleep. It was your last experience—and the starting point of a nightmare where the dream version of me was choking you."

"Exactly. I didn't even realize I was sleeping. It was as though my brain had erased the memory of spraying myself with the drug, and then my surroundings took a dark turn. That's how it works every time."

"And you're suggesting I give this horrible drug to my mother?"

He shrugs. "If she *can* be scared into waking up, this would do it."

"But what if she can't wake up? With the nightmares escalating, she'll end up in the worst hell imaginable, with no way out."

"Then you have to wake her using your power, after all." He doesn't bother hiding the disappointment in his voice. He must've wanted another subject to test the drug on. "Speaking of your power," he continues, "do you mind another experiment?"

I stare at him warily. "Like what?"

He stands up. "I'd like to see what happens if I withdraw my consent."

"Oh, that's fine."

He nods and scrunches his face, tensing—

———

I FIND myself back in the waking world, in the empty room where Dr. Cipactli is lying on the bed.

Looks like gnomes *can* take away their consent for dreamwalking—impressive.

Dr. Cipactli opens his eyes and sits up. "That was fascinating."

"Yeah," I say with a lot less enthusiasm.

"Can we do another experiment?"

I gesture to activate my comms and glance at my messages.

Valerian just replied, and I'm eager to know what he said.

"I'm sorry, maybe another time," I tell Dr. Cipactli. "I hope what we did thus far is payment enough for your time." *Especially considering how unhelpful you were,* is what I don't add.

"Fair enough," he says. "If you ever need a job, please keep us in mind. Someone with your powers could be invaluable when—"

"Thanks. I appreciate the offer. First, though, I need my mom safe and sound."

"Of course. If I can think of anything that might help her, I'll let you know."

We exchange contact details, and he leads me out.

As I walk out of the building, I finally read Valerian's terse response:

Let's talk. Can you meet me at Erato's at four?

Responding in the affirmative, I jump into a car and have it drop me at the hyperloop station. Erato's is on the other side of the city, so I need a speedier mode of transportation.

The hyperloop station in the Health District is typical for Gomorrah, in that it would put the poshest airport on Earth to shame, both in terms of the sleekness of its design and the comfort for the waiting passengers.

Not that we have to wait long. The train arrives every few seconds.

When I get on it, it's pretty empty. As usual, I can barely feel anything as it zooms forward and transports me the distance of ten Manhattans in an eyeblink.

Another car ride later, I step into Erato's building and ride the glass elevator to the top.

Erato is a powerful dryad who channeled her love of plants into vertical farming, making it something of an art form. The glass walls of the elevator allow me to ogle plants of every color and shape that cover every surface of the building. They're not just visually pleasing; the scents are divine as well, and the gorgeous nuts, fruits, and vegetables that peek out of the foliage make my mouth water.

I've got to hand it to Valerian. He picked a great place for our meeting—and a romantic one at that.

Maybe I'm not the only one affected by that crazy chemistry I've been feeling.

When I step out of the elevator into the restaurant, I feel like I'm in a magical forest. A green-skinned dryad dressed in a leaf bikini greets me with a smile that reveals her tree-root-like teeth. "Bailey?" she asks in a voice that sounds like autumn leaves falling.

I nod, looking into her chlorophyll-filled eyes.

"Come this way." She leads me through the thick greenery, her powers effortlessly commanding the branches to move out of our way.

The booth she leads me to looks like a miniature forest meadow with a large tree stump serving as the table, and smaller ones as chairs.

Valerian is already here, sitting on a stump and sipping a beaker of tea. Spotting me, he stands up and smiles.

I suddenly feel overly warm. Those sensual lips should be illegal, along with that chin dimple and the rest of that perfectly proportioned face. Not to mention that tall, muscled body... I remember the illusion he gave me the last time we met—that of him naked and covered by a glistening liquid—and it's all I can do to contain my drool. Thankfully, he's not naked right now, though the green tunic he's wearing might as well have been painted on. Not that he didn't look crazy hot in the bespoke suit he sported on Earth. He looks hot in everything—but especially in nothing.

That's actually a flaw in the idea that occurred to me earlier.

He's going to be a massive distraction.

He notices my staring, and his ocean-blue eyes gleam brighter, his grin turning wicked. "I'm glad you reached out," he murmurs as I plop gracelessly on the nearest stump. Even his voice brims with sex appeal. "I was afraid that after the clusterpuck that was the last job, I'd never hear from you again."

I swallow to moisten my dry throat. "Well... I appreciated the double payment." I'm still staring at him, I know, but I can't help it. Something about him looks familiar, always has. I have no idea where I could've met him, though. Initially, I'd thought that as an illusionist, he made himself look like a mix of celebrities, but then I learned that's not the case.

This is the true Valerian in all his mouth—and other body part—watering glory.

Finally tearing my gaze away from him, I activate my comms, so I can see the augmented reality menu through my new contacts. After a few seconds of deliberation, I select a mix of different teas and an appetizer fruit sample bowl—all species unique to this place.

"Hazard pay," he says dismissively when I'm done. "Did you already spend it and need more?"

"Not exactly." I disable the comms so nothing obscures my view of him. Immediately, my drooling resumes, so I hide it under a brisk, businesslike tone. "I'd like to run a theory by you."

His dark eyebrows arch.

"In Bernard's dream, I saw you speaking to your VR company and had an epiphany. You're planning to leverage giving VR to humans to grow your illusionist powers, right?"

His eyebrows rise higher. "An impressive deduction. No wonder you solved the case of the murdered Councilors."

I think I solved that case because I got lucky, but I'm not going to tell him that—the higher his opinion of me, the better. "So you don't deny it?"

A dryad arrives with a tray and puts a beaker of tea next to me, then sets down two identical fruit bowls.

Valerian grins. "We got the same thing. Great minds think alike."

I wait for the dryad to leave and for my heart to recover from the hormone-induced spike. Talk about a killer grin—if I were elderly and frail, I might've keeled over already. "So am I right about your plans?" I press when my voice is steady enough.

"More or less." He takes a round fruit that looks like Earth's guava and bites into it with gusto.

I fight an uncharacteristic urge to lick up the fruit juices from around his mouth. "In that case, I want in," I say and grab my own version of the same fruit before I can do something totally unprofessional, not to mention unsanitary.

Biting into the fruit, I taste its sweet, yet somehow

savory goodness, and my heart resumes racing as I notice him eyeing the juices around *my* mouth with a hungry expression.

My licking-things-up idea must be contagious.

"What do you mean?" he murmurs, his attention still on my lips.

I pick up my tea beaker with unsteady hands. "I want to grow my powers with the help of your VR company." I take a deep breath as his gaze snaps to mine and sharpens. "Your plan is to become associated with the illusory worlds of VR so that you become, in a way, a lord of illusions in human minds. I want you to let me do the same. Virtual reality can be dreamlike, so with the right game or app, I can be seen as a mistress of dreams—and therefore, my powers should grow. In theory."

I half expect him to laugh in my face and walk away, but he looks thoughtful instead. "One of the games we're developing features an illusionist hero," he says slowly. "Given how similar our powers are, that means the nuts and bolts for a dreamwalker character already exist. If we added some dream-related levels and your likeness as an alternate character…"

Oh, puck. I almost jump up in excitement. "You'll do it?"

His eyes gleam like blue diamonds. "I could—but it is a big ask. As beautiful as you are, I'll need something in return."

CHAPTER FIVE

I BLINK AT HIM, shell-shocked. He, this gorgeous creature, thinks I'm beautiful? Me?

The glow from the compliment almost obscures the other part of his statement: that I'd have to pay for my request. Now that I'm thinking about it, though, is it wrong that I hope he asks for something inappropriate as payment—say, my body?

"The Senate asked me to look into a certain classified matter for them," he continues, "and I could use someone with your investigative skills to help me out."

My horny bubble bursts. The Senate is the main governmental body on Gomorrah—which, unlike the Councils elsewhere, is elected by a democratic process. Going by what I've heard in the media, a classified investigation for the Senate might be an extremely dangerous undertaking.

I take a sip of my tea to calm myself. "I've just barely

survived one investigation. What do they want you to figure out? I can't help my mom if I'm dead."

He frowns. "What's wrong with your mom?"

I put down the beaker. "It's a long story."

"Tell me." He grabs a blue fruit reminiscent of an orange and peels it.

I hesitate for a second, then tell him everything: how Mom got into the accident and how the medical bills drove me to accept jobs of dubious legality, including his. I also explain that the healing Isis performed was incomplete and that I now need to get more power so I can wake Mom from inside her dreams.

As I speak, Valerian's chiseled features soften, and as I'm wrapping up my explanation, he covers my hand with his big, warm palm. "I'm sorry," he murmurs. "I'm glad those jobs I gave you helped out."

I resist the urge to pull my hand away—in part because I like his touch and in part because he's being nice and I don't want to insult him by implying he has cooties. Though he totally does. In his case, though, I weirdly don't mind it too much.

I bet even his cooties are hot.

I clear my throat. "This investigation, how long do you think it'll take?"

Before he can reply, the dryad comes back with two plates and what must be the second part of his order— a selection of vegetables in nut-based sauces.

Valerian deftly divides the food between our two

plates and tastes a mushroom-like morsel. "Delicious," he breathes, his eyes closing in ecstasy.

The dryad beams at him. "Erato will be pleased with your praise."

I feel a sudden urge to choke an innocent server, for no reason at all. I mean, all she did was smile at Valerian. Would I rather women be depressed around him?

Hmm. Maybe.

The dryad leaves, and I try my own version of the mushroom.

The thing is so foodgasmic a moan escapes my lips.

When I blink open my eyes—I didn't realize I'd closed them—Valerian is watching me with a hunger that has nothing to do with produce.

My face turns hot, my heartbeat ramping up. "You never answered my question," I mumble around a mouthful. "How long is the investigation?"

He peers at the greenery all around us, as if seeing other patrons and servers through the foliage. Then he refocuses on me. "I've just given us privacy with my powers," he explains. "If the waitress comes back, she'll see us eating and exchanging trivialities about the weather. Meanwhile, we can do anything we want and no one will be the wiser."

Nearly choking at the thought of doing "anything I want" with Valerian, I locate a juicy, broccoli-like stalk and stuff it in my mouth.

He watches me chew with evident fascination

before finally answering my earlier question. "I have no clue how long the investigation will take."

Ignoring my disappointed grimace, he locates his own version of the plant that I just ate and attacks it.

Watching his jaws move, I realize this process *can* be fascinating—I have an especially hard time keeping my eyes away from his mouth. With effort, I marshal my wayward thoughts. "How about you tell me what exactly we'll be investigating?"

He swallows his food with obvious pleasure. "That's classified. Without clearing it first with the Senate, there's not much I can tell you."

"Good thing we have privacy, though." I spear a giant bean with my fork. "Wouldn't want someone to overhear the nothing you just told me." I put the sauce-drenched bean in my mouth. Just like everything else so far, it's divine.

Peeling his eyes away from my mouth, Valerian says, "The mere fact that I'm investigating something is need-to-know information. I only told you because I trust you."

I narrow my eyes. "I wish that were mutual."

"You don't trust me?" He makes boyish puppy eyes —and it's unclear if he uses his powers to make me melt at the sight, or if his control over his face is that good.

A short fantasy plays in my head, one where he and I reproduce and have a boy child who makes those exact eyes at me to get a pony made out of chocolate frosting.

Wait, what? What am I thinking?

I grab the beaker and slurp the tea loudly to banish the insane thought. "What about the game development?" I ask. "How long do you think that would take?"

He smiles. "I'd need to talk to my team to find out for sure. I know this much: The Illusion Scope—the hardware for our games—is going live in a few days, along with a couple of games, so my team is stretched thin. The game in question is phase two, so lower priority." He makes short work of his own giant bean—as in, the legume, not the part of his body my mind keeps drifting to.

Tamping down on my unruly libido, I ask, "Would it be possible to make it higher priority? Maybe have your team start working on the changes to the game in parallel with your investigation?"

He raises an eyebrow. "As in, you want to get your payment before the job is even done?"

"Why not? You just said you trust me. Either way, you don't have to release the game until I finish the investigation. I just want to help Mom as soon as possible."

He gives me a dazzling grin. "You've got chutzpah, I'll give you that." Forking something that looks like a bright orange asparagus into his mouth, he consumes it with that signature relish of his.

I cross my arms in front of my chest. "Is that a no?"

"If you take all the money I've ever paid you and put a few zeroes at the end, that's about how much it would cost to do what you ask." He devours another morsel.

I edge forward on my stump-chair. "What if I helped with the game development?"

Mouth busy with the largest veggie on his plate, he gives me an incredulous look.

"I took courses in video game design," I say defensively. "On top of that, dreamwalking and game design are quite similar—and I have lots of experience with the former."

He chews thoughtfully, clearly not convinced.

"A good friend of mine also took those same courses. What if I convince him to help as well?"

Valerian swallows his food, his expression unreadable.

Possessed by some inner demon, I blurt, "He and I are *not* romantically involved."

Now he looks amused. "You should've led with that. He suddenly seems perfect for the job."

I tap my fingers on the stump-tabletop. "Felix is a wizard with computers. Literally so—he has power over silicon on top of his deep knowledge of computer science."

Valerian's gaze sharpens. "Is he that technomancer everyone hires to do their cyber security?"

"I think so. He certainly calls himself a technomancer." I give him a level look. "He owes me a favor, and I think I can get him to help."

That's a fib. If anything, I owe Felix a favor—or several. Still, I think I can convince him to lend a hand.

In the worst case, I could pay his usual rates—assuming he'd accept payment in Gomorran cc instead of US dollars.

"Fine." Valerian extends his hand. "You've got a deal."

With almost no hesitation, I grasp his palm. Cooties or not, his handshake is strong and firm, his skin pleasantly warm and dry as his palm engulfs my fingers. A part of me never wants to let go, even though the knowledge of the germs we're sharing freaks me the puck out.

A few loud heartbeats later, I realize we're still holding hands—and that he's gently massaging my palm. Whoa. His thumb is rubbing in the exact spot where my palm feels tense, and it feels both soothing and—

Something chimes in Valerian's pocket.

Frowning, he lets me go and makes a gesture that looks like a VR command. "That was my alarm," he says apologetically. "I have an important meeting I have to get to."

Flabbergasted by the handholding, I just nod.

He rises to his feet. "Get Felix on board and meet me at my headquarters on Earth later today. I'll send you the time and the address."

I nod again, still mute.

He makes a few gestures that look like he's taking care of payment, then leans in and brushes his lips over my cheek.

My heartbeat goes supersonic. Openmouthed, I

stare as he exits my personal space and strolls out of the restaurant as if he has no care in the world.

When he disappears from sight, I hygieia my hands and face and gulp down the rest of my tea before mindlessly devouring the rest of my food. Though everything is as delicious as before, the overactive state of my parasympathetic nervous system prevents me from enjoying it. Finishing the meal, I open up the app to pay and find that Valerian already paid for my portion.

That's nice of him. It's as if we were on a date. Wait a minute—were we?

Shoving aside the unsettling thought, I leave the restaurant and retrace my steps, taking the hyperloop and then a car to the hub building.

When I get into the elevator, I check my messages.

As promised, Valerian sent me the deets for our meeting.

I memorize the location in case my comms stop working when I get to Earth—though I doubt they will. Strictly speaking, I should leave all Gomorran tech here, but I'm feeling daring today. The New York Council owes me one, so even if I get caught, I'll probably get off scot-free.

Hopefully.

Exiting the elevator, I take in the view from the top of the skyscraper and bid civilization farewell. With a few decisive strides, I enter the pulsing energy of Earth's gate and arrive in the hidden section of the JFK airport. A few labyrinthian corridors later, I join the human travelers who have no idea this airport can take you to another world.

First things first: I find a place that sells hand sanitizer and get a few bottles. With no access to hygieia, this is the best I can do.

Ready to face this germ-infested world, I head for the taxi pickup location and text Felix on my Earth phone: *Need to talk to you in person.*

His answer comes back instantly: *Come to my apartment.*

I reply in the affirmative and use an app on my phone to summon a ride. Soon after, we hit traffic, my least favorite aspect of this place—besides the lack of proper sanitation, that is. On Gomorrah, we share the cars, which, combined with hyperloop and flying vehicles, has made traffic a thing of the past.

Eventually, we arrive in Manhattan.

Battery Park, the neighborhood where Felix lives, is nice—at least for Earth. There's lots of greenery all around, and the views of the toxic waters of the harbor are pleasing to the eye. When I get up to Felix's floor, it's bullet—and maybe even rocket—proof, something that's not the case with other apartments in the building.

I ring the doorbell.

CHAPTER SIX

THE DOOR OPENS, revealing Ariel's grinning face.

Ariel is an uber, an extremely good-looking and super-strong type of Cognizant. She and Felix are roommates, so seeing her here isn't a big shock.

"Bailey!" Before I can blink, she envelops me in a hug so tight a bear would be proud of it.

Since she doesn't touch any exposed skin, I find it easy to calm myself after the contact—especially once I catch my breath and ascertain that my ribs aren't broken.

"What are you doing here?" she asks excitedly, waving me in. "I didn't think you'd come back to Earth so soon after the last adventure."

"I'm surprising myself, trust me." I close the door behind myself.

Three furry creatures come out from the kitchen area and look up at me with varying levels of curiosity.

One is a chinchilla, an adorable rodent who isn't

what he seems. From our last encounter, I know that this is a domovoi, a rare type of Cognizant that are extremely powerful in their limited domain. His name is Fluffster, probably on account of all that fluff.

Hi, Bailey, he says as a voice in my head. *Good to see you again.*

Smiling, I return the greeting and examine the second creature, a cat of the Persian variety. Though she's not a Cognizant of any kind, there's a royal air about her, and the kind of evil intelligence in her eyes that makes me want to avoid getting on her bad side.

The third animal is another chinchilla, which prompts me to ask, "You got another pet?"

Ariel rolls her eyes. "We didn't. That's Kit."

"Oh, hi, Kit." Kit is a shapeshifter, and a powerful one at that—so much so she's on the New York Council. She can obviously be any creature crazy humans keep as pets, be it a chinchilla, or a dog, or a hippo.

I'm not a pet, Fluffster says in my mind, managing to "sound" grumpy.

"Sorry." I do my best to keep a straight face. "I meant 'another pet besides the cat.'"

The cat gives me a look that seems to say, "In reality, they're all *my* pets."

The extra chinchilla shimmers and transforms into Kit's petite, anime-like blonde form. "I'm here to keep Fluffster company," she says with a wink.

"Don't ask," Ariel whispers. "They're friends with disturbing benefits."

I don't actually see a problem with such an arrangement—apart from this being potentially bad for Kit's sex addiction. Ariel is a product of a world where anyone enjoying intimacy always looks humanoid, so I can't blame her for the bias. We're more open-minded on Gomorrah. Besides shapeshifters—who are rare— we've got a plethora of weres, and other Cognizant regularly hook up with them in various forms.

"What brings you here?" Kit asks and turns herself into Felix. "If it's to see the technomancer, he's busy with someone else at the moment."

"His girlfriend," Ariel clarifies conspiratorially. "I'm still getting used to the idea of him having one."

Not liking the look Kit gives me, I say, "Felix and I are just friends." Her expression doesn't change, so I add, "Not the kind of friends you and Fluffster are."

"That's good to know," says an unfamiliar female voice.

A beet-red Felix and a tiny young woman step into the living room. She looks familiar—this is the girl I've seen him defend from pucks in his dream, I realize.

"Maya, this is Bailey," Felix says. "We go way back."

Maya extends her hand to me, and I have no choice but to shake it, making a mental note to sanitize soon.

She peers at me through her glasses. "Felix said you took video game courses together, but he never mentioned how pretty you are."

I grin at her. "Thanks. Video game development is why I'm here, actually. Felix, can you help me add levels and features to a VR game?"

"Why?" he asks.

"What are you up to?" Kit inquires.

More questions follow from everyone except the cat, and bit by bit, I bring them up to speed about my mom, Valerian, and the deal we made. To avoid talking about my plan to gain power, I just tell them that Valerian will help me in exchange for some services that include the game.

"Valerian is ambitious," Kit says when I finish. "Releasing his VR headset and applying to be on the Council at the same time? I have no idea how he's juggling it all."

I frown. "He applied to be on the Council?"

"Wants to replace Hekima," Kit says, her face turning into the late illusionist's grandfatherly visage. "Will likely succeed, too. His predecessor proved just how powerful their kind can be—a boon to the Council."

"I still can't believe I took classes taught by someone capable of all those murders," Maya mutters. "He seemed so nice."

She took classes with Hekima?

Oh yeah, that's right. He taught something called Orientation here on Earth—a sort of school for the young Cognizant.

This Maya must not just look like a teen—she *is* one. I hope Felix knows what he's doing.

Felix directs a guilty look at Ariel. "A chance to work on VR. Maybe I could—"

"No," she says sternly. "We need you."

I raise an eyebrow.

"Felix can't help you," Maya says with a little too much eagerness. "His other friend from Gomorrah has dibs."

Is she jealous of me? If so, why? Her boyfriend is roommates with Ariel and Princess Peach—both more attractive than I am.

Deciding to ignore her, I look at Felix skeptically. "You have *other* friends on Gomorrah?"

"Itzel," Kit explains and turns into the person in question: a round-cheeked young gnome with a goofy smile. In the real world, that smile would be hidden by a mask, since Itzel, like all of her kind, suffers from breathing issues.

"What's wrong with Itzel?" I ask, worried. She's a friend of mine as well.

"It's her famous grandfather," Ariel says.

Famous is an understatement. Cadmael singlehandedly boosted the quality of life on Gomorrah to the levels we currently enjoy. In his youth, he invented a reactor that provides energy that's almost free and therefore powers every aspect of our day-to-day life.

"What did he do this time?" I ask in exasperation.

For as long as I've known Itzel, her grandfather has been a pain in her butt. Recently, for example, he acquired a gambling debt so large that Itzel had to take a risky job to help Felix and his friends. She was so traumatized from their adventure that she asked me to treat her with dream therapy—which I intend to do at some point in the near future, since I now know how to enter gnome dreams.

"He disappeared off the face of Gomorrah," Felix says. "Itzel asked us to help, and we owe her."

"Of course," I say. "And I'd like to help too."

Everyone except Maya looks happy at the news—though it's hard to tell what Fluffster is thinking under all that fur, and the cat's flat face must always look a little bit grumpy.

What about your mother? Fluffster asks mentally.

Momentarily forgetting about cooties, I reach down and pick him up.

Wow. The risk of disease is worth it. Chinchilla fur is almost as heavenly as Pom's.

"My mom takes priority, of course," I reply, looking into his rodent eyes. "But I'm hoping the video game stuff and my payment to Valerian won't occupy all of my waking time."

I don't add that I'm beginning to miss vampire blood. With this much going on, sleep is a luxury. But I'd better resist these thoughts; it could be addiction rearing its ugly head. If my waking time isn't enough for people, they can bite me. Especially Valerian—that way, I might even enjoy it.

Felix grins. "Awesome. We'd love your help—and maybe I can still help you with the game when *I* have free time."

I put Fluffster back on the floor. "That would be great. Maybe you can do it in place of some of your paid gigs. I'll pay your usual rate."

At the mention of money, Fluffster puffs up. *Felix will gladly help you. Itzel's favor isn't going to pay rent or put groceries into the fridge.*

"But he can't do it *now*," Maya says. "We're going to Cadmael's apartment so I can use my powers to locate him." She puts her tiny hands on her hips. "I only have a short window of time when I'm free, so we need to go. Right now."

"Right," Felix says sheepishly. "We'd better leave."

Funny how this rush seemed to materialize only when I did. I decide against saying anything, though; Maya will be even more certain that I want her boyfriend, which I don't.

All my amorous thoughts are directed at Valerian as of late.

I look at Felix with a stony expression, lest Maya thinks I'm undressing him with my eyes. "Before you go, can you give me an update on Leal's comms?" I glance at Maya apologetically. "Leal was a dreamwalker whose murder the New York Council asked me to solve. His comms contain his notes and may provide useful information about my powers."

Felix perks up. "Oh, yeah, forgot to tell you. I was able to hack those. Got his whole journal. Checked on Soma, as you asked—no mention of it. He did seem obsessed about some secret society that's like the Illuminati but on steroids. At least that's as far as I got before I grew bored."

It's all I can do to conceal my disappointment. I was really hoping there'd be something about Soma in

Leal's notes. Hekima had implied that it's a place where dreamwalkers live, but it's unclear if he meant a city or a whole Otherland.

Thanks to my mom's secretiveness, I know so little about my kind—or my family. She's never even talked about my early childhood years—which sucks, since I don't remember anything from before I was seven.

Ariel cocks her head. "A secret society?"

"Yeah," Felix says. "A group called Icelus."

Kit morphs into Leal and rolls his/her eyes. "That again? He brought that up in front of the Council a few times. A ridiculous notion." She turns back into her usual self. "According to him, Icelus are a cult of Cognizant worshipping some weird god."

Ariel looks intrigued. "Like the Brotherhood?"

"The monks are not secret about their faith." Kit turns herself into one of the hooded figures.

"Right," Felix chimes in. "Unlike the Brotherhood, Icelus hide their affiliation—and their deity isn't very nice. Leal says Icelus are behind some terrible things here on Earth."

Kit scoffs. "Delusions of an old man. He claimed they started wars and invented terrorist acts. His list went on and on. There's no way a group of Cognizant could've gotten away with all that under the noses of the Councils."

"Unless they'd infiltrated the Councils," Felix says. "Which is what Leal claimed. He even—"

"Can I get the notes so I can read them myself?" I glance at the door. "You're in a rush, remember?"

"Right." Felix disappears into his room and comes back with the dreamwalker's antiquated comms.

I take out my own shiny new model and my local phone. "Send them to one of these, please."

Felix snatches my new comms out of my hands and examines them with the excitement males usually save for the female form.

Maya scowls at me.

"Where are the glasses for this thing?" Felix asks. "And the gloves?"

I explain about the invisible headphones, the contacts, and the nails. Felix looks so enthralled I half expect him to have an orgasm, while Maya's scowl grows into a death glare.

"I think I'm going to get these once we find Itzel's grandfather," Felix whispers reverently.

I blow out an exasperated breath. "Do what you wish. But send me the files now, okay?"

"Oh, right." He shoots both devices with an arc of his technomancer energy. "Done."

I turn on my VR and see a new message with an attachment. I open it to find many pages of text.

Fine. I'll read this when I have more time.

Maya possessively grabs Felix's elbow. "We'd better go."

"Good idea," I say. "I'll get in touch with you through Itzel once I'm back on Gomorrah and have a free moment."

As Ariel and the others put on their shoes, I double-check when I need to meet Valerian and do the math on how long it'll take to get to his company's offices.

I have about an hour to kill.

"Can I hang out with Fluffster here?" I ask Felix and Ariel.

"Of course," Ariel says and hugs me without warning.

Before I can recover from her hug, Kit does it to me as well.

Maya coldly waves goodbye, and Felix cautiously shakes my hand.

I wait until they exit, then run to the bathroom to sterilize myself with soap and hand sanitizer. Feeling as clean as is possible without hygieia, I return to the living room and chat with Fluffster until it's time for me to leave.

One day you should come when I'm sleeping, the domovoi tells me as I head for the door. *I'm curious to experience your powers.*

"Deal." Unable to resist, I pet his heavenly fur. "See you later."

CHAPTER SEVEN

IN THE CAB, I sanitize the hand that touched Fluffster's fur and open Leal's journal.

Oh boy. There's a lot of boring stuff here—experiments on his poor birds and pages upon pages of stream of consciousness on mundane issues, including such gross bits as records of his bowel movements.

I search for Soma as a keyword and find nothing, just as Felix warned me.

Disappointed, I settle in and just read. Eventually, I come across what Felix mentioned—paranoid-sounding ramblings about a secret society.

They worship Phobetor, the lord of nightmares. They think him a god. Does he exist? If so, what is he? Could he be a creature that is to Cognizant what we are to humans?

I try to parse that paragraph:

There are worlds where we, the Cognizant, are worshipped as gods. In fact, this happened in the distant past of Earth too. For example, Loki, the god of mischief, was a famous probability manipulator. But what would it mean for some being to be a god to us Cognizant?

The cab stops next to a shiny building, interrupting my musings.

I ride to the top floor, where a large "Bale Inc" plaque proudly announces the name of the company, and approach the front desk.

"Mr. Bale, your guest is here to see you," the receptionist announces into her phone.

Valerian comes out wearing another bespoke suit. Puck, he looks good in it. Like, cover-of-fashion-magazine kind of good.

Oh, and he must be the Mr. Bale she was referring to. That's why the company is Bale Inc.

Huh. So if I married Valerian and followed the antiquated coverture custom of taking the husband's last name, I'd be Bailey Bale.

Not sure how I feel about that.

"Where's the technomancer?" Valerian looks around as if Felix could be hiding in a corner somewhere.

"Turns out he has another commitment." I put my hands in a praying position. "Please don't renege on the deal."

He sighs. "How about you join us in the meeting room?"

I follow him into a big, glass-encased space where two other men are waiting at a glass conference table. One I already know, I realize—a mustachioed guy who looks like the video game character Mario, but with a scar on his forehead.

It's Bernard, the human Valerian commissioned me to "inspire" in his dreams. It's the job Valerian paid me that nice bonus for—as he should have, now that I'm thinking about it. Not only was I busted by the New York Council while doing it, but the job itself was quite complex due to Bernard's endless trauma loops. The poor guy lost a child to a monster, then himself became monstrous in his revenge.

Looking at him now, you'd never be able to tell what happened. He's the very picture of a mild-mannered software engineer. I wonder if he's a psychopath on some level, or if what he did lives in every parent, ready to be triggered by a horrible-enough stimulus.

The other man I've never met before, and it's a shame.

Despite being waif thin, he's almost as attractive as Valerian, with similarly symmetrical masculine features and strong dark eyebrows. His hair is pure black, and his skin tone is similar to mine.

"Bailey Spade, please meet Bernard Anderson and Ratridevi Bhairava," Valerian says and sits down.

"Nice to meet you, Mr. Anderson," I say to Bernard. "And you, Mr. Bhairava."

"Please call me Bernie." Bernard smiles. "Because of the *Matrix* movies, I never go by Mr. Anderson."

Another fan of that franchise. He and Felix would

get along—particularly if I never tell Felix about Bernie's gruesome past.

"I also don't go by my last name," Mr. Bhairava says with a slight Indian accent. "Please call me Rattie."

I blink at him.

"It's a play on Ratri, the short version of my first name," he explains. "People here find it easier to say it that way."

Well, okay then. If he doesn't mind that nickname, so be it. For what it's worth, he doesn't look at all ratty. If I had to compare him to a rodent, I'd say he looks more like a very handsome beaver. Or an otter, though that's no longer a rodent. Or even a *cheburashka*—a koala-like creature that lives in the preserved equatorial jungle on Gomorrah.

"Do I also have to come up with a nickname?" I ask, plopping into a sleek office chair.

Could I go by Bails? Or Beernuts?

Valerian sits down. "No need. We don't *all* go by nicknames."

I salute crisply. "Fair enough, *Mr. Bale, sir.*"

A sensuous smile tugs at the corner of his lips. "I do let those close to me call me Valerian." His voice deepens in a way that sends a tendril of excitement into my nether regions—an awkward situation, especially in front of Bernie and Rattie.

Taking a deep breath to settle my speeding pulse, I pull my sleeves down to cover Pom's fur—it's turned an embarrassing coral pink.

Valerian, meanwhile, is back to being all business.

"Do you want your teams dialed in?" he asks Bernie and Rattie in a brisk tone.

"Not yet," Rattie says, and Bernie concurs.

"Fine." Valerian looks at me. "I've already explained the idea to them. You're going to be the model for a project we're calling *Lucid Dreamer*."

Rattie grins at me. "I convinced them that instead of this being a new character in an existing game, a new standalone VR game experience makes a lot more sense."

"One that uses the foundational work of the other projects," Bernie chimes in. "To deeply cut on prerequisite resources."

I drum my fingers on the glass table. "A new game? Does that mean it'll take longer?"

"In a way, yes," Valerian says. "But there's also good news. Rattie thinks his team could have a working level in a matter of days—between their Trembling in the Dark project and everything else, they have almost everything they need. It's just a matter of stitching bits together."

Trembling in the Dark? I heard about it from Felix. He said, and I quote, "It's the scariest horror video game of all time."

"So *Lucid Dreamer* will be scary?" I ask Rattie.

He shrugs. "If the game is about the mistress of dreams, I figured why not have her fight nightmares? Especially since my team is so good at that sort of thing."

"Valerian recently purchased Rattie's whole studio,"

Bernie explains. "They've been helping out on everything, but they want to sink their teeth into a game of their own."

"Which means a thousand-plus people will be working on this," Valerian says meaningfully.

Oh, puck. No wonder he said this is a big ask; the budget must be in the millions.

Bernie opens his mouth to speak, but his phone rings. He surreptitiously glances at the screen, and a tender smile appears on his face as he takes the call.

"Hi, honey, thank you so much for calling me back." Muting his phone, he looks at us apologetically. "It's my daughter. We haven't spoken in years. I'll be right back."

Valerian nods and Bernie takes the phone out of the room.

So they reconnected? In his dreams, it was something that tormented Bernard—I mean, Bernie. Perhaps having gone through his trauma loops under my watch, he feels better and has reached out to his family?

"Let me answer this for Bernie," Rattie says. "We'll obviously need to figure out more of the story than simply 'fight nightmares,' but given my team's expertise and that Valerian wants the game bumped to phase one, this is the smart play."

"Right," I say, feeling a bit overwhelmed. "Whatever can speed this up sounds good to me."

Bernie comes back with an apology.

Ignoring him, Valerian gives me a knowing smile. "I

never finished explaining why having a working level is good news. We have testers equipped with the Illusion Scope prototypes, waiting for something to play. There are twenty thousand of them, and growing." He looks at me pointedly.

I stare back at him blankly; other than being even more impressed with the budget he's throwing at this thing, I don't see what the special good news is.

Disembodied letters suddenly appear in the air in front of me. They look like LEGO pieces and form a paragraph of text—clearly the work of Valerian's illusion powers:

When thousands of humans play that demo, your powers will get a boost—I know this from personal experience. Not as big a boost as when the game goes live, obviously, but a noticeable one. If you're lucky, that boost might be what you need to best your mother.

Wow. I was settling in for a wait that would span months, but it turns out I might be able to save Mom in a matter of days.

I beam at him. "This is great news indeed. What can I do to speed this up?"

"I got that part," Valerian says to Rattie and Bernie. "Get in touch with your teams before Bailey and I leave."

We're leaving? Okay then.

Rattie presses a button on the side of the desk, and a bunch of giant screens slide from the ceiling and cover the walls. A video conference app chimes, and soon every screen displays the enthusiastic faces of hundreds of people—most likely developers, designers, animators, audio engineers, and so on.

Please introduce yourself and we'll go, Valerian tells me via the LEGO text.

"Hi, everyone," I say, looking into the cameras. "My name is Bailey, and I will be the model for the *Lucid Dreamer* project. I also happen to know something about game design, so I'd be happy to help in any way I can—just let me know what you need when you need it." I keep going in that vein, eventually starting to sound like an army general psyching his troops for an attack.

"Thank you," Valerian says when I finish my speech. "Why don't we go to the motion capture lab so we can get started?"

Everyone applauds and waves to me as we leave.

I feel pleasantly odd, as if I just took a tiny sip of diluted vampire blood for the first time.

Am I high on being involved in game development, or is it Valerian's proximity?

As we enter the elevator, I notice him watching me intently.

"I feel strange," I blurt. "In a good way."

Valerian presses the button for the fifteenth floor. "There's a chance your powers got boosted by merely having that many humans believe in you as the game model for a dreamwalker-related game," he says in a low voice. "When my own power got boosted, I felt very peculiar." He closes his eyes, as if in bliss, and I store that expression in my memory banks for use in the dream world.

I imagine that's what his O-face looks like.

The elevator opens, and we enter a room with green screens for walls and enough computer equipment to oversee a space launch.

Valerian picks up a small piece of cloth from a chair and hands it to me. "Put this on."

It's a onesie-like outfit made from a blue material with big gray dots. I look at it, then at him.

Nope, he's not kidding. He actually expects me to wear it.

I heave a sigh. "Where's the fitting room?"

An amused gleam appears in his ocean-blue eyes. "Why?"

I don't justify that with a reply.

"I'll just look away." Matching actions to words, he turns his broad back to me.

At least I think his back is to me. He can be using his powers to make me *think* he's looking away, while in actuality, he's standing there with a magnifying glass directed at my privates.

Then again, where do I draw the line when it comes to paranoia? He can just as easily use his power to make himself invisible and stand in any fitting room—like he did the other day in the bathroom while I showered.

It's a recollection that should enrage me, but it makes me feel warm and tingly instead.

Without further ado, I strip off my clothes and pull on the onesie. It's stretchy, so it fits.

I look at Valerian's back.

There's a tension in his shoulders that I choose to interpret as him suffering with the effort not to turn around and gawk at my awesomeness.

"Done," I announce.

He turns around and grins at me before going to a nearby table to pick up a bunch of objects that look like the dots attached to my outfit.

"I need to glue these to your face," he says, approaching me.

"You what?"

"They're sterile, I swear," he says, and before I can object, he attaches the first one to my forehead, the tips of his fingers brushing over the skin around the dot.

Holy digitization. I had no idea my forehead was an erogenous zone.

He attaches another dot to my forehead, then another.

My breathing turns shallow.

Valerian grins, his eyes gleaming wickedly, and starts gluing dots to my nose, cheeks, and near my lips. By the time he finally attaches a dot to my chin, I feel like I need a change of panties.

Leaving me utterly discombobulated, he goes to set up the primitive Earth equipment.

"Can you follow instructions?" he asks with a smirk.

I clear my dry throat. "What do you need me to do?"

He asks me to display different emotions with my

face, and I do my best—sometimes doing such a good job that Pom changes color on my wrist to match the expression. He then asks me to move for him, directing me this way and that. The weird part is that I find all this bossing around kind of hot—and not just the parts where he asks me to sway my hips and things like that.

Hours of motion capture later, Valerian says, "That's enough. We should be good for the demo, but might need you back after that."

I hold my breath as he carefully removes the dots from my face and turns his back to me again.

I shake off my hormone-induced daze and slip out of the onesie. Before putting on my original outfit, I use up all of my remaining hand sanitizer on my face and body—because that's the rational thing to do.

However much it turns me on, I can't forget that Valerian's touch is full of Earth germs.

"I have some business on Gomorrah," he says when he turns around. "But you should stay and work with Rattie and the team for as long as you can. In fifteen hours, though, I'll need you for the first part of the Senate investigation, so meet me back at Erato's then."

Erato's? "We're eating there again?"

He shakes his head. "In fifteen Earth hours, it will be midnight on Gomorrah. Instead of dining, we'll be invading Erato's dreams."

"We?" Is he including himself in this dreamwalking adventure?

"We'll talk details after you make a dream link and

get away from Erato's dwelling. I assume you can dreamwalk in a dryad?"

"I don't see why not, but—"

"Good. Let's go."

He leads me back to the elevator, and as he presses the button for the top floor, I recall something I've been meaning to ask him. "Does the word 'Soma' mean anything to you?"

He stiffens for a second, then his expression smooths out. "Can you give me some context?"

"It's something Hekima mentioned in his last moments," I say, puzzled by his reaction. "He made it sound like a place where dreamwalkers live. It also sounded like at least one illusionist family lived there too—Hekima's own."

Valerian's jaw tightens. "You can't trust anything that murderer said."

"So you don't know?" I ask—though it's obvious to me that he does.

"I'm sorry. I can't help you with this."

"But—"

"If you want me to keep helping you, drop it," he growls just as the elevator doors open.

Fine. If he's going to ask me nicely like that, I guess I won't pry anymore.

He strides back into the meeting room, and I follow. Bernie and Rattie are there, but instead of the teleconference, the screens feature drawings of bone-chilling monsters and mind-bending environments.

Clearly, the work on the demo is proceeding at breakneck speed.

"My team is extremely excited," Rattie says to Valerian. "I already have some stuff I want to run past you."

Valerian holds up his hand. "I have a prior commitment, but Bailey can serve in my stead." He glances at me. "I trust her implicitly when it comes to the *Lucid Dreamer.*"

As Valerian leaves us there, Bernie looks at me dubiously, but Rattie doesn't bat an eye. "So, Bailey," he says, "in your opinion, when in someone's dream, should the dreamwalker character actually walk? Some folks suggested she fly or teleport around."

"Let her walk," I say. "If dreamwalking were real, I imagine all of the above would be possible, but she might still walk by default as that's what's familiar and doesn't require extra effort and concentration."

"Logical," Rattie says. "And no flying cuts on dev time."

"We haven't done flying in VR before," Bernie adds.

"Flying also has a higher chance of giving the gamer VR sickness," I say, without sharing why I think so. There are flying games on Gomorrah that did that to me—and I'm an experienced flyer, at least in my dreams.

Rattie peppers me with more questions, and I answer as best I can, drawing on my game design knowledge when I need to, as well as on dreamwalker experience.

After a while, Rattie yawns in the most contagious manner. "I think it's time for a few hours in the pod," he says apologetically. "I'm still on Bangalore time."

Bernie stifles a yawn of his own. "It's not your jet lag. I could use some time in the pod myself."

Catching the bug, I can't help but yawn too. "What's this pod business?" I stretch to banish the sleepiness.

Rattie stands up. "Game development is a crazy business. We often work so much there isn't time to go home and sleep."

"Which is why we installed sleeping pods here at the New York offices," Bernie says, rising to his feet as well.

I look at each man in turn. "You sleep on the job?"

Rattie shrugs. "When it's needed. Usually during crunch times."

I nod, then yawn again.

"We have a pod not assigned to anyone," Bernie says. "It's yours if you want a power nap." Seeing me cringe in disgust, he adds, "It's brand new. You'd be the first person to use it."

Curiosity getting the better of me, I agree.

Rattie leads the way until we reach a room filled with the aforementioned pods—which look like a hybrid between a rocket and a coffin.

Rattie opens the clear plastic lid of one of them. With a wave, he lies down, shuts the lid, and closes his eyes.

"This is the pod I mentioned." Bernie points at one that does indeed look brand new.

"Thanks," I say. "I just might use it."

Bernie smiles and heads over to a pod that has a picture of a child glued on the inside. I recognize the image as that of his daughter—I've seen her in his dreams. Climbing in, he mumbles something about sweet dreams and closes the lid.

Huh. I never realized game development was such hectic work that you don't even get to go home to sleep. I think I might stick to dreamwalking as my primary career, after all—at least once I save Mom.

Setting my alarm on "vibrate" so I don't wake up others, I climb into my own pod and close my eyes.

CHAPTER EIGHT

THE VIBRATION of the alarm wakes me.

I feel groggy, like I could sleep for many more hours. Oh, well. Maybe I'll sleep after I help Valerian with the Erato business.

Climbing out of my pod, I notice Bernie and Rattie are still slumbering in theirs. I approach Rattie and check his eyelids. Yep. He's dreaming right now. That means I could establish a dream link with him if I wanted to.

It doesn't take me long to decide. I *do* want to. I could then inspire him when it comes to levels of my game, for starters.

Stealthily lifting the lid, I touch Rattie's forehead.

———

I APPEAR in my dream palace and come face to face with Pom.

"Bailey," he exclaims, turning a deep purple. "I've missed your face."

I fluff his fur. "Can't you just make yourself a dream version of my face and stare at it in a pinch?"

To demonstrate, I create a disembodied replica of my grinning mug and leave it floating in the air next to me.

He gives a small shudder. "That looks kind of disturbing."

I roll my eyes. "Good to know. I didn't realize my face has that effect on you."

"When not attached to the rest of you, it gets creepy," he says seriously. "I guess your arms and legs keep your face from being that way."

Shaking my head, I teleport to the tower of sleepers and look for Rattie.

He's indeed in a nook, not far from Bernie, who's also showed up in his bed.

"Trauma loop," Pom says, the tips of his ears darkening as he eyes the clouds above Rattie's head.

He's right. And not just any clouds, but turbulent ones. I rub the tip of my nose. "I don't get it. Does Valerian seek out software engineers with deep psychological trauma, or is it just bad luck on everyone's part?"

Pom's fur darkens further. "I'm not going in there with you."

"I don't think I'm going in either. I have to meet Valerian and do a job for him in the waking world. I've set up a link with this guy so I can inspire him in the future, not deal with that." I wave at the clouds.

"Inspire him?" Pom turns light orange. "Are you talking about the private things you do with Valerian that you asked me not to witness?"

I put my hands on my hips. "First of all, I never got further than first base with Dream Valerian. Secondly—"

"What's first base?"

"*Secondly*, that is not the kind of inspiration I'm talking about. Besides, Rattie might be pleasant to look at, but doing stuff like that with him would feel like cheating on Valerian, even in dreams."

Wait, what am I saying? How can you cheat on someone when you're not in a relationship?

Pom takes on the colors of root vegetables—first a carrot, then a beet. "Did I upset you?"

"It's fine." I sigh. "The private stuff you mention is a sensitive subject, that's all."

He waggles his ears. "Like the P word for me?"

The P-word stands for "parasite"—which Pom contends he's not, preferring "symbiont" instead. Of course, considering that he uses me as his food source, feels my emotions, possibly excretes his metabolic byproducts into my blood stream, and is attached to my wrist to the end of our days, the jury on parasite-versus-symbiont is still out.

He bristles. "I can't believe you just thought that."

"I was just testing if you're reading my thoughts. You said you wouldn't, but you did."

He turns a deeper shade of beet. "Sorry. I'll stay out of your thoughts going forward."

"Thanks." I fluff his fur. "And we're definitely symbionts."

His ears perk up. "Like a bee and a flower?"

"Definitely *not* like a bee and a flower," I say and jolt myself out of the dream world.

———

STRUGGLING NOT TO GIGGLE, I open my eyes next to Rattie's pod. Though it's unclear which of us Pom views as the flower, I know this much: If anyone's going to do any pollination of me, it better be Valerian.

Speaking of which, I need to get moving, else I won't make it to Gomorrah on time. I leave the building and buy more hand sanitizer before grabbing a taxi to JFK. Once we hit the inevitable traffic, I open up Leal's journal in my VR view to have another look.

Skimming over a lot of minutiae, I locate something that piques my interest:

Another day, another failure. I'm beginning to think touchless dreamwalking is impossible—or if it is possible, it may be something only those of us with more power can master.

Touchless dreamwalking? How does that work?

I search the journal for more mentions of this term and eventually puzzle out that it's basically a way to enter someone's dream from a short distance—in lieu of touching them skin-to-skin.

Puck, that would be amazing. My least favorite thing about my powers is all this exposure to cooties. Next time I meet a sleeper, I'll see if I can do this.

Arriving at JFK, I make my way to the secret hub and enter the gate that leads to Gomorrah. Once there, I stop by my place to use the bathroom, change my clothes, hygieia myself from head to foot, drink like a camel, and scarf down some manna. Then I head over to my destination—Erato's restaurant.

Valerian is already there, waiting for me by the building.

He's changed his suit for an outfit that would definitely look out of place on the parts of Earth I'm familiar with. It's a black, sporty bodysuit, a skintight contraption that shows off every muscle on his body as thoroughly as if he were naked and covered in tar.

Another flush heats my skin. This outfit will definitely make it hard to concentrate on the job, whatever it is.

Valerian's clearly not in the mood for flirting, though. "You're late." He puts on a breathing mask that blocks his features and makes him look like a gnome, then hands the same thing to me. "Put this on."

Before I can ask any pertinent questions—such as, "What the puck are we doing?"—he stalks into the building and summons the elevator.

I hurry after him, fitting the mask on the way. "Wha—"

He places a finger to where the lips would be under

the mask, and the LEGO letters show up in the air: *My powers can't fool listening devices if they're there.*

I nod in comprehension, and we ride the elevator in silence. When we get to the hundred-and-fifth floor, Valerian steps out, and I follow, staring at our surroundings in awe.

The walls are covered from floor to ceiling with vertically growing plants, each one with a dedicated lamp and a mist machine nourishing it.

"I feel like we're in a greenhouse," I whisper.

Don't talk and stay in the middle of the corridor, he tells me via LEGO letters.

Demonstrating what he means, he keeps away from the walls as he creeps forward.

I mime his actions as closely as I can, though I doubt my movements achieve the predatory grace of his.

He stops next to a moss-covered door and waves an unfamiliar device over a lock. There's a click, and the door slides out of our way. He takes out another gizmo and tosses it inside.

That will disable all electronics for a while, he tells me via LEGO letters.

I nod.

He waves for me to follow and moves even stealthier, which is logical since we've now officially broken into someone's lodgings.

Bringing up my VR, I write him a message: *If we get caught, will the Senate pardon us?*

Stern-looking LEGO letters show up in the air immediately: *Never refer to this job in electronic messages again. And to answer your question: it would be easier for them to make us disappear, so let's not get caught.*

Great. Just great. *Now* he tells me that.

Sighing, I follow him deeper into the apartment, which reminds me of the restaurant—a veritable jungle of different plants of all shapes and sizes. Only unlike the restaurant, there's a sinister quality to some of the vegetation—like the acid seed okra, a flowering plant that can open its pods and spit out seeds up to two hundred feet. Those seeds, as the name implies, are covered with a powerful acid. And that's an unmodified plant. Others appear to have been engineered from their nasty natural brethren, like the one that looks like poison hogweed—a plant covered by deadly poison, only with thorns. There's also a cousin of the famous strangle vine, only bigger. The winner of the creep show, though, is sitting in a giant pot in the middle of the room. It's a distant brother of the bug trap flower, except it's big enough to eat a person instead of a bug.

Press here, Valerian's LEGO text informs me as he touches a button on the right cheek of his mask.

I do the same, and the scent of the air coming into the mask changes, becoming more sterile. It must be getting filtered.

Valerian takes out a sleep grenade.

Interesting.

Gliding through the plants like a jaguar, he stops next to a door and quietly opens it before tossing the grenade inside.

Touch her to make a connection, he orders a few seconds later. *If she wasn't asleep, she should be now.*

Doing my best not to make any sounds, I slink into the room and examine the sleeping dryad inside.

Based on her reputation, I figured Erato had to be older, but I didn't realize she was downright ancient. Her green hair is almost entirely gray, and the green skin of her face looks like weathered tree bark.

Watching her eyelids, I frown.

What are you waiting for? Valerian asks.

I point at her lids, then at the eyeholes of my mask as I rapidly move my eyes to explain what I need.

So we're just going to stand here until she starts dreaming?

Since I don't know how to pantomime "I don't want to risk going homicidally crazy," I pointedly shrug.

With a barely audible sigh, he crosses his arms over his broad chest and closes his eyes.

Ignoring his pouting, I switch my attention to Erato's eyelids.

Nothing.

I bring up my VR display and set a timer for the length of time it typically takes for the gas to leave a large person's system. If this small woman doesn't go into REM sleep by the time the alarm rings, I'll have to risk dealing with the subdream. Hopefully I won't have to, though. The last time, with my mom, was brutal.

Feeling like the worst cat burglar in the history of thievery, I open Leal's journal in my VR view and look for something interesting to read. I still haven't found anything by the time the VR alarm rings, so I close the journal.

And that's when I realize something odd is happening in the room.

All the plants around us seem to be coming alive and moving with an eerie purpose.

She's in REM sleep, Valerian informs me.

I glance at her eyelids. She is indeed, and she must be dreaming about something that makes her agitate the plants.

I carefully approach her bed and extend my hand. Before my fingers touch her leathery skin, I remember the power I recently learned about—touchless dreamwalking—and decide to try it.

Keeping my hand extended, I will myself to go into Erato's dream.

Nothing happens.

I strain so hard a vein pops in my forehead.

Still nada.

The way the plants move grows spookier.

What's the holdup? Valerian asks. *Make the connection, and let's get out. You'll do the actual dreamwalking once we're safely away.*

Fine. Maybe now isn't a good time for experimentation.

I touch the dryad's green forehead and go in the

regular way, popping in and out of the dream palace before Pom has a chance to say hi.

Task accomplished, I nod at Valerian and pull my hand away. "Let's go," I say quietly—which is when the dryad's eyes open and the plants around us coil for a strike like an army of snakes.

CHAPTER NINE

PUCK. I cast a frantic glance at Valerian. Why isn't he conjuring up some illusions to save us?

I made us invisible to her senses, he says, reading the panic on my face. *But her plants are aware of us somehow, and I don't know how to fool them.*

Plants with senses? I guess that makes sense. How else are they able to lean toward light or grow roots downward into the soil instead of in some random direction?

"Is someone here?" The dryad sits up, and the plants move with greater purpose, tendrils and branches reaching out like arms.

Grasping my hand, Valerian begins to tiptoe out of the room.

The dryad leaps naked out of the bed, grabs a knife, and starts slicing at the air.

Valerian drags me out of the bedroom.

Midway through the living room, a strangle vine snakes from the ceiling and wraps around my neck. Gasping, I flail my limbs as it pulls me up. Valerian rips at the vine, but all this does is slightly loosen its grip so I suffocate slower.

"Whoever you are, you're not leaving here alive!" Erato shouts, running out of the bedroom. Her gaze is still blindly sweeping the room, not noticing us thanks to Valerian's powers.

Suddenly, she looks directly at me.

Puck.

Knife ready, she lunges at me. The blade slices an inch above my head, cleaving the vine holding me.

As I fall into Valerian's arms, I understand what happened. He made Erato see whatever she needed to see in order to strike where she did—and to accidentally free me from the vine.

He must still be showing her whatever it is because she growls in anger and leaps to the center of the room as Valerian lowers me to my feet.

We run for the door.

The poison hogweed swipes at me, its thorns missing my face by a hair's width.

Pucking puck. Remind me to never break into a dryad's home again.

I glance back and see Erato stumbling into the deadly embrace of the bug trap flower. The flower's giant trap closes, muffling the dryad's confused cry. Before I can celebrate our narrow escape, the pods of the acid seed okra turn toward me, moving as if in slow motion.

I don't even get the chance to think the word "duck" before an acid seed flies at my chest like a bullet.

CHAPTER TEN

ONLY IT DOESN'T SMASH into me. With the speed a Secret Service agent would be proud of, Valerian yanks me behind him, taking the projectile in the chest in my stead.

The material of his outfit begins to sizzle, and terror rips through me. Pucking idiot! What was he thinking? Who made him my bodyguard? I want to yell at him, but there's no time. Hands shaking, I grab my hand sanitizer and squirt the cleansing liquid at the spot where the acid is attacking Valerian's suit.

The sizzling seems to lessen.

Valerian tears at the front of his suit, ripping a chunk away.

There's a nasty burn on his chest, which I squirt with more hand sanitizer.

I'll live, he informs me via LEGO letters. *We have to go.*

Grimacing in pain, he grabs my hand and pulls me

toward the door as Erato's knife slices open the side of the bug trap.

We sprint for the elevator. Erato is on our heels, and the plants in the hallway try to stop us—except these are regular, non-deadly plants, so they fail.

As he summons the elevator, Valerian must spare a second to make Erato see something that isn't there because she hurls her knife in the direction opposite us.

We leap into the elevator, and he punches the button for the roof.

The doors close, shutting out the dryad, but I don't exhale until we get all the way to the top, where a flying car is waiting for us. As soon as we jump inside, it lifts off the roof.

I rip the stupid mask off my face and squirt more sanitizer at the burn on Valerian's chest. He won't die, I know that now, but I'm still furious that he took that kind of risk.

"What were you thinking?" I say through gritted teeth. "You could've—"

"It's okay." Removing his own mask, he covers my hand with his. "It doesn't hurt anymore."

"But why did you even—" I stop short because he pulls out a small vial and takes a sip.

His eyes close in that blissful O-face expression, and the wound instantly heals.

I narrow my eyes at the vial. "Vampire blood?"

He puts it away. "I only use it in case of emergencies."

I take a deep breath, some of my fury abating. If he had that with him, then he wasn't in as much danger from the acid seed as I thought. Still, the idea that he took that deadly projectile for me...

"Don't do that again. Ever," I say grimly. "The risking your life for me part, I mean. And be careful with that blood."

He arches his eyebrows. "I'm always careful. Do you have a problem with it?"

"I almost did." I tell him about my recent troubles with that highly addictive substance, and when I finish, he takes out the vial and demonstratively pours it out the car's window.

"No need to have that sort of temptation around you," he explains. "I don't need it that much."

Before I can process that, the car descends onto a landing strip on a rooftop. Distracted, I peer at it. It looks like a private rooftop, in which case Valerian is even richer than I thought.

We land, and as we exit, he tells the car not to expect us for a while.

I blink up at him. "It's your personal car?"

Most citizens of Gomorrah share rides—both driving and flying ones—which is how we don't have traffic the way they do in New York and other Earth cities. Only one percent of the richest one percent bother with private rides.

He lovingly pats the shiny surface of the vehicle. "Sometimes you order a ride, and it takes time to arrive."

"Sure. It makes sense to spend a fortune to avoid wasting those valuable milliseconds."

He grins and leads me to the elevator.

Surprise surprise. We only descend one floor, to the penthouse of this skyscraper—the most expensive dwelling you can imagine. He waves his hand, and the shiny black door quietly slides open, revealing an expansive loft-like space with twenty-foot-high ceilings made almost entirely of glass.

Talk about skylights.

That's not what makes my breath catch in my chest, though.

Someone put a thirty-foot-wide water pond here, smack in the middle of the penthouse.

Is this real? I've never seen such a thing. Then again, I guess if you can have a pool, you can have a pond—if you're into throwing money away, that is. Unless this thing is an illusion, Valerian must own the floor below this one just to make room for the bottom of this body of water.

As I come closer, I see a few swamp flowers that have multicolored legu sitting on them—frog-like amphibians that squeak instead of croak.

It's a whole pucking ecosystem, and a nice one at that. The scent of the flowers, their colors, the sounds of the water splashing, and the little squeaks all seem to be carefully calculated to pleasantly stimulate the senses.

"This is not an illusion," Valerian says before I can ask. "There's also ri living in the water."

Sure enough, I spot the little fish-like creatures. They look like rubies with fins and tails.

Valerian takes off his shoes, sits on the edge of the pond, and dips his naked feet into the water with a contented sigh. Catching my gaze, he grins and pats the spot next to him.

I gingerly crouch there.

"You can put your feet in." He curls and uncurls his toes, clearly relishing the feel of the water. "It's nice."

I grimace. "No, thanks. I could live my whole life without soaking my feet in the same place those legu and ri go to the bathroom."

"Your loss." His expression turns serious. "Are you ready to go into Erato's dream?"

I get more comfortable by twisting my legs into a lotus pose I learned in a yoga class on Earth. "Sure. What am I looking for when I'm in there?"

"Right." His gaze is intent on my face. "I have to tell you what the Senate asked me to do."

Finally. "Go ahead."

"How much do you know about Icelus?" His voice tightens on the last word.

Icelus? Is he talking about the secret society cult from Leal's notes? The one Kit dismissed as the dreamwalker being delusional? "Well," I say slowly, "allegedly, they did some bad things on Earth and—"

"What the puck do you mean by 'allegedly?'"

I scoot back, startled by his vehement reaction. "I don't know. During my investigation for the Council, I got Leal's journal—you know, the dead dreamwalker?

—and he'd made claims about Icelus that sound like conspiracy theories. Nobody on the Council took him seriously, so..."

Valerian's forearm muscles flex, like he's fighting not to clench his fists. "Whatever heinous crimes Leal accused them of, Icelus are guilty of far worse."

I give him an incredulous stare. "Worse than wars and terrorist acts?"

He nods grimly. "Their goal is to maximize the number and frequency of nightmares everywhere to serve their deity."

Huh, okay. Maybe Leal wasn't all that delusional. "That deity being Phobetor, the god of nightmares?"

"Do *not* utter that name," Valerian snaps. "Just like the nightmares, it gives him power."

Wait, what? Is Phobetor like Voldemort, He Who Must Not Be Named? Actually, I don't think Harry Potter's nemesis got more power when his name was said out loud. Either way, why does Valerian sound like he believes the same mumbo-jumbo as Icelus?

There's no way there's such a thing as Phobetor.

"I won't do it again," I say reassuringly, just in case. "How about I call him something safe, like Collywobbles? In English, that means stomach pain or queasiness."

"I know English well," Valerian says, his gaze softening slightly. "I've been on Earth more than you."

"Oh?"

"I immigrated there a while back."

I scooch back toward him, driven by curiosity. "What about your parents? Did they also immigrate?"

"No." His features darken. "Icelus took them from me before that."

The torment in his eyes makes my chest ache, and on my wrist, Pom turns darker than a black hole. Unbidden, my hand reaches out and rests reassuringly on Valerian's stiff shoulder.

"I'm so sorry," I murmur.

His shoulder minutely relaxes. "It was a long time ago." Eyes glinting, he adds, "The killer paid dearly for what he did."

No doubt. I don't even want to imagine what kind of horrific things Valerian can do with his powers to someone he hates.

He places his palm over mine, his gaze growing heavy-lidded.

Wow. His touch is like the heat of an exploding quasar. It spreads through my body and settles somewhere low in my core.

I snatch my hand away before I do something crazy, like lean over and plant a kiss on those sensuous lips. "Back to the Senate job."

"Right." His features grow taut again. "Since the government here knows of their existence, Icelus have been very careful when it comes to their operations on Gomorrah—until recently, that is. The Senate have reason to believe that Icelus *are* plotting something here, and they've asked many people, me included, to look into it."

"And that dryad—"

"Is the reason the Senate needed *me* for that part of the investigation. Because of some of the horrific genetically modified plants she recently patented, they think she's an agent or at least a lead to one, but they don't want to spook her. They want me to use my powers to extract the information from her without her realizing they're on to her, but I think your powers will work even better."

I massage the bridge of my nose. "You don't think our little visit spooked her?"

"Hopefully not. As we were flying, I got the Senate to replace the surveillance footage in her home and the rest of that building. When she checked it, she saw herself running around like a madwoman."

I whistle. "Isn't that illegal?"

He shrugs. "The Senate decides what's legal."

"Right. So much for the rule of law."

He splashes at the water with his foot. "Do you have what you need for the dreamwalking?"

"No. I could use an anchor."

He raises an eyebrow.

"Something that would help me get the right dream started," I explain. "Saves a ton of time."

"Use her patent filings." He gestures around, clearly activating his comms.

I check my inbox. Yep. A message from him is waiting there, full of attachments.

As I review the plant designs, a shiver goes down my spine.

These make the man-eating plants from her apartment seem like cuddly kittens.

The tamest one is a tree with blooms that remind me of corpse flowers native to Earth, but uglier. The pollen these trees produce would be toxic enough to fell even a vampire. With the right wind, a single tree could wipe out whole neighborhoods.

"She's insane," I mutter as I review more of the deadly flora.

"Icelus seek to create nightmare fuel whenever they can," Valerian says. "Even someone writing an article about these plants can be helpful to them."

"No kidding." I turn off the VR. "I myself might have a nightmare about a garden with these abominations. Do you think Icelus plan to unleash these plants on us?"

"That's what I want you to find out," he says. "Will those filings work as an anchor?"

"Only one way to find out." I rise to my feet. "Please don't disturb me as I go into my trance."

I don't know why, but I turn away from him before I touch Pom. I guess I still don't trust him with this information.

Hand resting on my looft's soothing fur, I dive into the dream world.

CHAPTER ELEVEN

I FIND Pom in the lobby of my dream palace, shooting a laser gun at targets that remind me of inter-Otherland gates, only with a shimmering bull's eye in the middle.

A pang of guilt bites at me. Before all my problems started, I'd regularly play competitive games with Pom, everything from tennis to fencing. They'd brought my little friend incalculable joy, and were fun for me also. Now I've ignored him for so long, he's been forced to play with himself.

But not in a dirty way.

Probably.

Hopefully.

"Bailey!" Pom makes his game accoutrements disappear and flies around my head with the enthusiasm of an overcaffeinated puppy. "What's going on?"

I take a slow route to the tower of sleepers so I can bring him up to speed.

"And that's her? The dryad?" He looks at the green newcomer in one of the nooks.

"Yep." I fly over to her bed. "Looks like she was able to fall back asleep."

He lands on my shoulder. "Can I join you in her dreams? Doesn't seem like it'll be very scary."

"Just don't give away our presence," I say and make us both invisible as I reach out to touch Erato's forehead.

———

ERATO IS LYING naked on her bed. A nearby shrub extends a cucumber-like fruit toward her groin.

Before Pom and I witness something we'll never be able to unsee, I change the plant into a giant VR screen.

Despite the incongruity, the dryad doesn't wake up. Good. I put the plant designs from her patents on the screen, and she focuses on them, as I hoped.

With her attention occupied, I change the room around us to be more generic, then clothe her and make sure she's standing upright.

This is it. If this is close enough to a memory—and intuition tells me it is—she'll take care of the rest. And she does. The room starts to look like her living room, except the front door is different.

Suddenly, the door in question breaks into tiny pieces, and a giant wolf leaps through what remains.

With a flash, he turns into a naked male with Elvis-like sideburns and a Mohawk hairdo popular with gremlins.

Anger twists Erato's features. She recognizes him.

"Stupid bitch," he growls. "Which part of 'discreet job' was unclear to you?"

Three strangle vines snake from the ceiling. One wraps around the guy's throat, and two grab his wrists. "Now," Erato says menacingly, "what were you saying?"

The guy sneers. "If something happens to me, the people I work for will have your spleen."

Erato waves a hand, and a poison hogweed coils within a hair's width from his feet. "Given your lack of intellect, I doubt you're as indispensable as you think."

"Test it and see," he snarls.

She waves her hand again, and the acid seed okra pod zeroes in on the guy's torso. "I don't have to kill you, you know. Something tells me if I make you look even uglier, the people you work for will thank me."

Interesting. It doesn't sound like they're part of the same group. Does that mean she's not Icelus?

"The patents," he grits out. "How could—"

"I patent all of my creations," Erato says calmly. "I offered you exclusive rights, but it was outside your budget."

He shows his teeth. "I didn't realize that was what we were talking about."

"Didn't realize. Didn't think." She taps her temple. "Are you beginning to see a pattern here?"

In a flash, the werewolf turns back into his wolf form.

A wall of greenery rises between him and Erato.

"If something happens to me, a letter will go to the Senate," she says. "If you work for who I think you do, that's the last thing you want."

He growls and bounds back through the door, disappearing from sight.

The dream stops being a memory at this point as some of the plants turn into green creatures that don't exist, at least not on Gomorrah.

Figuring I have enough info to share with Valerian, I leave the dream world.

———

HE'S STANDING RIGHT NEXT to me as I emerge from the trance, close enough that his bacteria could easily jump on me if they wished. And he's staring at my face like a dermatologist looking for a scary mole.

I instinctively step back, flushing all over.

He cocks his head.

I dampen my lips. "Were you staring at me that whole time?"

"Not staring," he murmurs, his gaze briefly dipping to my mouth. "Admiring."

My flush deepens. Clearing my dry throat, I say, "Ready to hear about Erato's dream?"

His expression turns serious, and I tell him what I just saw.

"That makes sense," he says.

I blink at him. "It does?"

"The Senate had two theories for why Erato would file those patents. One was that she's with Icelus, and the filing was designed to give nightmares to the clerks at the patent office and others in the know."

I scratch my eyebrow. "Sounds like too much trouble for relatively few nightmares."

He nods. "This is why I think their second theory must be the right one. She took that job from Icelus but filed the patents to mitigate the damage her work would actually do."

"Oh?"

"If someone were to use those plants for a terrorist attack, the Senate would already have countermeasures in place," Valerian says. "And I bet Erato knew that would be the case—which is why she filed in the first place. No wonder her employer was so pissed."

That does make sense. "So what now?"

"Give me a second." He makes some gestures, querying something in his comms. "I can't seem to find a werewolf matching your description in the Enforcer database," he says after a moment. "He was probably in disguise."

I think back to the sideburns and Mohawk. "That might explain why he looked so odd."

Valerian makes a few more VR gestures. "I'm going to use my powers on you in a second, if you don't mind."

Before I can actually say if I mind or not, the living

room goes away, replaced with a giant stadium. All around me stand people with different faces but the same Elvis sideburns and Mohawks as the werewolf in the dream. Each wears a name tag, as though this were an orthodontist convention.

"I'm showing you every werewolf on Gomorrah who has a record." Valerian's disembodied voice seems to be coming from every direction. "I added the hair to make it easier for you to identify the one from the dream."

I nod, and the werewolves begin to parade in front of me, each giving me a good chance to have a look at his face.

After about an hour of this, I yawn.

"I'm sorry," Valerian says from everywhere. "I wish I knew a faster way to do this."

"I could show him to you in a dream," I say, looking at the sky.

"Just a few more suspects," he says. "Then you can go home and rest."

The werewolf parade continues in the same vein until I spot a guy who might be the one.

"Him," I say when he gets closer, and I know for sure. "Hans Stubbe."

"Are you certain?" Valerian asks.

"His sideburns were longer, but it's him. I'm positive."

The stadium and all the werewolves except Hans go away, leaving me back in Valerian's living room.

Valerian shifts his gaze from something in his VR

display to me. "Based on his profile, he's probably a hired gun instead of an actual Icelus initiate."

I yawn. "Do you know where we can find him? Because if not, I know a guy."

"Yeah, leave it with me." Valerian makes Hans go away. "By tomorrow night, I'll have the location."

"In that case, I'd better go get my beauty rest," I say, suppressing yet another yawn. "I still owe myself hours and hours of sleep."

"You know," Valerian murmurs, eyes darkening, "you can sleep here."

My throat goes dry. "I'm not sure that's a good idea."

Wait. Why did I say that? It *is* a good idea. In general, why am I not all over him already? How long can I stay a virgin before it seems creepy? I may already be there, in fact. And if I were to lose it, I can't think of a better person to find it than—

He steps toward me. "I know you want to."

"You do?" I sneak a glance at my coral-pink Pom bracelet.

Is that what gave me away? Or is it something about the way I smell or look?

Instead of replying, he dips his head and presses his lips to mine.

Wow. Wow. Wow.

At first, I'm too shocked to do anything but process the sensations. His lips are soft and warm, their gentle, undemanding pressure making me crave more. But then unwelcome statistics flood my brain, the ones about the millions of bacteria we're already exchanging, even with our mouths closed.

If the kiss gets more intimate, our microbiomes will merge and stay that way forever and ever. And bacteria are just the tip of the frightening iceberg. Viruses such as herpes simplex or papilloma are also real possibilities—depending on who else Valerian has kissed before me.

I don't know if it's the idea that he's kissed others or my dread of germs, but I pull away from the kiss.

There's a hurt expression on his gorgeous face.

Puck. Did I pull away too sharply? And, germs aside, was pulling away what I really wanted?

Feeling like an idiot, I take a step back—and my foot plunges into the cold pond water. I squeal and flail my arms to regain my balance, but my other foot slips off the edge.

Valerian lunges forward and catches me, yanking me to safety.

As soon as I'm steady on my feet, he releases me, his face unreadable.

Mumbling a weak thanks, I beeline for the door, leaving wet footprints behind me.

———

MY EMOTIONS IN TURMOIL, I get into a car. Thank the stars it's self-driving. The last thing I want is to face a sentient being in my current state.

Once we set out, I exhale a frustrated breath. What

the puck was that all about? I've wanted to kiss Valerian ever since I first laid eyes on him, yet when he finally made the move, I totally pucked everything up.

Now he knows I'm a freak, the only woman my age who's never kissed anyone. I can only have intimacy in my dreams—and even there, not with a real person but a figment of my own imagination.

This is why I haven't dated. I'd rather face Earth's dentists than explain all this to a guy I like.

Needing to get my mind off the clusterpuck that is my love life, I open Leal's diary. Now that I have reason to believe he wasn't just a paranoid curmudgeon, I read his thoughts on Icelus with a lot more interest.

According to him, someone had been killing Icelus agents on Earth—a mystery person Leal felt great gratitude toward.

I freeze for a second, recalling what Valerian just told me about his parents. Could that have been him? Is he capable of being so ruthless? I picture his expression when he was talking about Icelus and realize the answer is yes.

I can imagine him taking out Icelus agents in all sorts of gruesome ways.

My chest tightens with sympathy again as I think about him dealing with the loss of both of his parents. I can't picture losing my mom. Even now, with her in a hopefully reversible coma, I feel like an orphan. How much worse would it have been for Valerian at that age?

Ugh, I'm a horrible person. He opened up to me,

telling me about this tragedy in his past, and I treated him like a leper because of my stupid germ issues.

Glumly, I return to the notes and skim through a bunch of boring stuff. But then I come across something interesting.

Leal claims that Icelus have a drug that puts people into REM sleep. He says it has a dire side effect but doesn't say what it is before going on about how invaluable to him such a drug would be.

Skimming further, I'm not surprised to find him talking about hiring someone to replicate said drug. I know he succeeded in that. Of course, his version also had a side effect, the worst possible kind. Whoever took his drug never woke up. That's what happened to Eduardo, the werewolf on the New York Council.

I continue to skim until a yawn overcomes me. Now that the adrenaline from the kiss is fading, my sleepiness is returning full force, and Leal's boring notes aren't helping.

Closing the journal, I open my messages and find Itzel in my contacts.

I can help you guys look for your grandfather tomorrow, I tell her. *Let me know where I can meet everyone.*

I send the message just as the car stops next to my building. The ride on the elevator happens in a sleepy haze, as does undressing and treating myself to hygieia all over my body.

When I finally get into bed, I'm asleep before my head touches the pillow.

CHAPTER TWELVE

AS I EAT BREAKFAST, I activate the VR and check my messages. There's a reply from Itzel telling me where to meet her and the gang on Gomorrah, so as soon as I finish my meal, I head out to Nebulabucks.

Nebulabucks is a teashop chain, and the location Itzel chose must be new—the line of thirsty Cognizant is only ten minutes long. Felix, Ariel, Itzel, and Kit are sitting at the biggest table in the corner, hot drinks in everyone's hands.

Felix holds out a cup to me. "Nebula flower, the way you like it."

Thanking him, I take the cup and sniff it as I sit down next to Ariel. The fruity notes of the tea are divine.

"How did your game development thing go with Valerian?" Ariel asks with an eyebrow waggle.

I flush at the reminder of the kiss fiasco. "Long

story." I look at Itzel's masked face. "Did you find your grandfather?"

"No," the gnome says, her nasal voice disguised by the breathing apparatus. "But we made some progress."

"Or Maya did," Felix says proudly.

I look around the table again, then peek under it. "Where's your little friend?"

"She's eighteen," Felix says defensively—and no wonder. I'm pretty sure he's at least in his mid-twenties.

Ariel grins. "Legal as of very recently."

"But do tell Bailey where she is." Kit turns herself into the petite girlfriend in question and gives Felix an evil smirk. "I'm sure it'll make it crystal clear how mature she is."

Felix glares at Ariel and Maya/Kit. "She's got a trigonometry exam."

Kit morphs into Felix. "*Advanced* trigonometry," she says in his voice. "Must not forget that."

Ariel's grin widens. "Still a high school subject. And no, it won't help matters if you tell Bailey about the advanced placement classes Maya takes."

"Come now," I say, my face exaggeratedly serious. "Maya sounds like a very bright young lady."

Felix slurps his tea very loudly, then says, "Anyway, this high school student was the only one who could help us make heads or tails of Cadmael's disappearance."

"Indeed," Itzel says sternly. "And if we could get back to said disappearance, that would be swell."

I turn my attention to her grumpy face. "What did you learn?"

"We found a vaping pen in Grandpa's apartment," Itzel says. "It didn't seem to be his, so we asked Maya to touch it."

"Her power is psychometry," Felix chimes in. "She can tell who an object belongs to when she—"

"We all know what psychometry is," Ariel says with an eye roll.

Itzel puts down her cup. "Do you want to see how it went?"

"Please." I take a big gulp of my tea.

Itzel puts on a set of VR glasses and gloves and makes a few gestures.

I hide my surprise at seeing that she has an older model of comms. Since she's a gnome, I expected her to have the latest gadgets. Then again, she might resent that stereotype, similar to how peaceful orcs dislike being perceived as violent brutes.

Opening my own VR interface, I click on the video she's just sent me.

———

THE VR PUTS me in a cluttered room, presumably in Cadmael's apartment. Maya is sitting on the floor next to dirty socks, holding the vape gizmo in her tiny hands.

A glowing, purple-tinted energy seeps from her skin into the object, and her expression turns trance-like. "He's punching an elf in the face," she chants under her breath. "Now he's punching a dwarf, then a—" Her eyes roll back. Then she exhales, and her eyes return to normal.

"His name is Vas Lube," she says, sounding tired. "He's an extremely aggressive orc."

So much for not stereotyping. Nobody around me looks surprised to hear of an orc's involvement either.

Itzel's voice rings out from where the VR camera must've stood. "Where can we find this orc?"

Maya shrugs. "I can only tell you who he is, not his location."

The VR recording terminates.

———

I DISMISS my VR and find myself back at the table in the teahouse.

"So it's safe to assume he took Cadmael," I say, looking at my friends. "An orc named Vas Lube."

Kit is grinning. "I hope Vas isn't short for Vaseline."

"Leave it to Kit to turn an orc's name into something sexual," Felix mutters under his breath.

I pick up my tea. "What did you guys do once you got the name?"

"Nothing," Itzel growls. "I don't know anyone who's ever heard that name. Nor do they." She sweeps her gaze around the table.

"It's a good thing you have me then," I say, "because I know a guy."

"Who?" Ariel asks, her eyebrows furrowing.

"I don't think you guys know him. I helped him out once, and now he helps me when I need something from the Gomorrah underworld." *Such as vampire blood* is what I don't add, since it might still be a sensitive topic for Ariel.

Itzel jackknifes to her feet. "Let's go see him now."

———

AS WE DRIVE to the bar where my guy—Napoleon—always hangs out, I ponder whether it wouldn't be wiser to ask Valerian for help with this instead. If he can locate the werewolf from Erato's dreams, he might also be able to find this orc.

Problem is, I'm not sure I can face Valerian after last night's debacle, let alone ask him for favors. In fact, I wouldn't be surprised if he were to find someone else to help him with the werewolf and disappear from my life for good. He's probably canceling the *Lucid Dreamer* project at this very moment, so even my mom will suffer due to my inability to kiss a guy I like.

"Bailey." Ariel touches my shoulder. "We're here."

And so we are. This is exactly the seedy bar we need.

Taking a few steadying breaths, I exit the car and lead everyone to our destination.

———

"THIS PLACE REMINDS me of the Mos Eisley Cantina from *Star Wars*," Felix whispers as we enter.

"All the bars and clubs on Gomorrah remind you of that," Ariel says. "You need to get out more."

Napoleon is sitting on an extra-tall barstool to the side, looking red, horned, and tiny, as usual.

I nod toward him. "That's my guy."

"Wait a second," Felix says. "I know him. He sold me a gun once."

I gape at him. Guns are extremely illegal here on Gomorrah, to the point that even the Enforcers—our law enforcement—are not allowed to carry them. Only the Senate Guard, a type of secret service for the government, and the Gomorrah equivalent of SWAT carry guns.

Then again, given what I know about Napoleon, it doesn't surprise me that he sells guns and other taboo items.

"What kind of Cognizant is he?" Ariel whispers loudly. "He looks like a little red devil."

I cast a worried glance at Napoleon. I hope his hearing can't pick up what we're saying. "He calls himself a nain rouge."

"That's just 'red dwarf' in French," Itzel whispers.

Of course she speaks French. Gnomes are very good at languages.

"I believe his kind are more commonly called the lutin," Kit says in a hushed tone and turns herself into a pretty and feminine little red devil. "They're forced to look like humans on Earth." She transforms into a petite human with the same features as the little devil. "The lutin are amazing lovers."

"Someone really needs to get laid," Felix mutters under his breath.

"You volunteering?" Kit shimmers into Maya and licks her lips in a disturbingly sexual manner.

Felix reddens to Napoleon's levels as Ariel chokes on laughter. At the bar, Napoleon's pointy ear twitches.

"Hey, Napoleon!" I call loudly and head toward him.

The nain rouge puts down his murky, ruby-colored drink and turns around to scan the bar. Spotting me, he bares his sharp, predatory teeth in a wide smile.

"Bailey." He pronounces my name with a district French accent. "Nice to see you outside my dreams for a change."

I smile and greet him in French before switching to English for the benefit of my American friends. "This is Kit, Itzel, and Ariel, and you already know Felix."

Napoleon looks Felix up and down. "*Oui*, the gun. I hope you only used it on your backwater world, as you assured me you would."

Felix bobs his head. "I'd never brandish it on Gomorrah."

"Good. Good." Napoleon picks up his drink and takes a sip. "I charge double the price I gave you if it's for local use."

Itzel huffs. "Worried if someone gets caught, it could come back to bite you?"

"Gnomes and their bluntness." Napoleon gulps the rest of his drink. "Even orcs have more finesse."

"Speaking of orcs," I say casually, hoping to keep the cost of the information we need as low as possible. "We're looking for one named Vas Lube. Where can we find him?"

Clicking his little red fingers, Napoleon summons the elf bartender and orders another drink—Chimera's Fire.

I inwardly cringe. He's about to get a concoction so hot and spicy, some say it's made by fermenting reaper peppers—abominations with a Scoville Heat Unit in the millions.

The bartender places the drink in front of Napoleon, and as a drop of it spills on the coaster, it sizzles.

The nain rouge takes a long sip and grins as contentedly as a child chasing a chocolate chip cookie with warm milk.

"So, about Vas," I say with exaggerated patience. "We need information."

Napoleon lowers his drink to study me. "I like you," he says, his breath smelling of pepper spray. "I don't want you to get yourself killed."

My friends and I exchange glances.

"He's dangerous?" Felix asks.

"As dangerous as they come." Napoleon looks around furtively. "He runs with the Filthy Bastards."

I glance at Itzel to see if she knows what he's talking about.

She looks just as blank as I do, and our off-world companions appear even more clueless.

Napoleon sighs deeply. "I'm talking about a gang that chose to name themselves Filthy Bastards. Do I really need to explain this further?"

Itzel's eyebrows snap together. "I don't care if they call themselves Abominable Rascals or Repulsive Reprobates," she growls, leaning into Napoleon's personal space. "This Vas person knows something about my grandfather's disappearance, and I intend to speak with him."

"Remind me never to let Itzel name a gang," Felix whispers. "Rascals?"

If Napoleon minds being face to face with Itzel's breathing mask, he doesn't show it. "Who's your grandfather?" he asks, seemingly offhandedly.

"You wouldn't know him," I say quickly. If Itzel mentions that her gramps is a famous inventor, the price of the information we seek will get a number of zeroes tacked on to it, if it hasn't already.

"By telling you what I know, I'll be putting myself at risk," Napoleon says right into Itzel's face. "I hope you're ready to compensate me accordingly."

Itzel's eyes water—probably from Napoleon's spicy breath. Wiping at her face with her sleeve, she steps back.

"How much?" I ask.

Napoleon names an insane figure.

"Throw in guns for each and every one of us, and you've got yourself a deal," Itzel says before I can even start to bargain.

He picks up his hellish drink. "I only have one gun left. And you'd have to use it off-world."

"We plan to use the gun when we face Vas," I say evenly. "Take it or leave it."

There's no way this is actually the last gun he owns, but if I challenge him on it, it'll do more harm than good.

Napoleon grins, exposing his fangs. "I'll take it... *if* you visit my dreams one more time."

Itzel better appreciate this. "At a time of my choosing," I say reluctantly. "And not soon."

"*Oui.* Just bear in mind, that time will need to be before you need my help again." He downs the rest of his drink, probably getting an ulcer right then and there.

We all chip in to pay for Napoleon's services, with Itzel insisting on contributing the lion's share. When we tell him to check his balance, Napoleon gestures in his VR like an opera conductor. Upon seeing the money in his account, he gives us a predatory grin and gesticulates a few more times before saying, "Check your messages."

Sure enough, he's sent us the location of the gang's hangout.

"Pleasure doing business with you," he says when I confirm I got the directions.

"What about the gun?" Itzel asks.

Grunting, he reaches under the bar in front of him and pulls out a sleek, short-musket-like device. Before anyone can see the highly illegal weapon and report us, I snatch it and hide it in the back of my pants.

We quickly hustle out of the bar and summon a ride. Itzel instructs the car to go to her place. "Felix's suit is there," she explains. "If we're going to look for a gang member inside their own hideout, we need all the help we can get."

———

ITZEL'S APARTMENT looks like a mad rocket scientist's lair. There are countless screens with rocket designs on them, half-built drones, tangles of wires, and jars of exotic fuels.

In the walk-in closet by the living room stands the suit in question—which looks like a sci-fi B movie robot.

"Felix claims he was inspired by the very first clunker of a suit built by Iron Man," Ariel says. "While I think he ripped off the Mech Batsuit."

Felix puffs out his chest. "This is a Neo Golem original." He launches into an explanation behind the name, which boils down to this: If Felix were a superhero, that would be his code name.

"So we have a gun"—I pat the back of my pants—"and the Neo-Golem suit. Anyone else feel like it's not enough?"

"Depends on how many of the so-called Filthy Bastards will be there," Itzel says. "I don't care, though. It's the only lead we've got."

I stroke Pom's fur. She's beginning to scare me slightly. "How about we swing by my apartment?" I suggest. "I've got sleep grenades there, which might help us avoid violence altogether."

Felix steps into his suit and snaps the robot-like faceplate in place. "Sounds good." His voice comes out muffled.

As we exit onto the street, Felix receives a few curious glances, but not as many as he'd get on Earth, outside of theme parks.

We take a car to my apartment, where we grab a couple of sleep grenades and a bite to eat. While we're at it, I ask Felix to teach me how to use the gun, since he seems to have the experience.

"Right." He takes the gun from me and presses a button on the side. An antiquated-looking screen shows up above the gun—clearly, this isn't a new model. He points at a self-explanatory label on the screen. "This controls if the gun's ray is lethal or not." He sets the gun to stun mode and aims it at Ariel.

"Ha-ha," she says humorlessly. "Suit or not, I can still break you in half."

With a huff, Felix points the gun at my window. "It's really this simple. Point and shoot." He mimes squeezing the trigger.

I take the gun and practice summoning and hiding the screen. It's as easy as Felix said. I stick the gun into the back of my pants. "Got it. Let's go."

We summon another car and head straight for the location Napoleon provided, which turns out to be a seedy-looking cul-de-sac in one of the worst parts of Gomorrah.

"At least no one will mind Felix's suit," Ariel says, wrinkling her nose as we step out onto a urine-stained street decorated by piles of never-picked-up garbage. It's beyond gross, even with the cool breeze that's blowing away the worst of the stench. I hold my breath the best I can, but the putrid aroma seeps into my nostrils anyway.

Itzel really owes me one. The germs here must be almost as bad as on Earth.

Napoleon's directions lead us to what once was a storefront but is now boarded up and missing a sign.

"No way to see what's waiting for us inside," Ariel whispers as she tries to peek behind the plastic covering the windows.

Kit makes herself look like an orc. "I could pretend to be a newbie who wants to join the gang."

"No," Itzel whispers. "Let's stick to Bailey's sleep grenade plan."

Nodding, I check the door.

It's locked.

I take out my lockpicks, but Felix puts a hand on my shoulder before I can use them. He then shoots the door with an arc of magenta energy. "In case there's an alarm," he quietly explains.

Still in her orc form, Kit eyes the door dubiously. "I don't think this place has functional indoor plumbing, let alone alarms."

I shush them and get to work with the lockpicks.

Everyone watches my hands in fascination. As soon as the lock gives in, I carefully open the door and toss in the grenade. Closing the door, I count the seconds in my head to make sure whoever's inside has fallen asleep and the gas has neutralized, letting us walk in safely.

"Hey!" a voice growls behind us. "What the puck are you doing?"

Startled, we spin around as one.

Scowling at us is a veritable army of Filthy Bastards.

CHAPTER THIRTEEN

"THEY MUST'VE SNUCK up on us as Bailey was dealing with the lock," Felix whispers, and everyone is too tense to chastise him for stating the blatantly obvious.

Ariel reacts first, her military training kicking in as she leaps forward and punches an orc twice her size in the chest. Her opponent flies back at his comrades, who stagger back before they catch him and shove him back at her.

Before I can see how Ariel fares, I spot a stone flying our way.

It smashes into Felix's metallic chest. His Neo Golem face shield goes up, and the robotic suit rips into the crowd of our attackers, making disturbing flesh-meets-metal smacking sounds along the way.

If it weren't for the breeze that would take the gas away too swiftly, I'd consider using my remaining sleeping grenade. As is, I yank out the gun, activate it, and aim it at the head of the nearest orc.

The gun beeps. Though nothing seems to come out of the barrel, the orc falls unconscious. The gun is still on the nonlethal setting—a good thing, as this orc may well be the one we seek.

"We just want to talk to Vas," Itzel shouts. "There's no need for anyone to get hurt!"

A Filthy Bastard with the perfect features of an uber spits at Itzel, and his saliva lands on her mask.

Puck. If that were me, I'd kill him for that unauthorized sharing of bodily fluids.

Itzel must feel the same. Eyes turning into slits, she forms a ball of lightning between her hands and hurls it at her assailant.

The guy flies back and crashes into his brethren, knocking them off their feet like bowling pins.

An orc takes his place.

Heart hammering, I render him unconscious with my gun and survey the rest of the battlefield.

Felix is battling a dwarf and an orc—and looks to be winning. Ariel is effortlessly beating up two elves. Still in her orc form, Kit is facing off with an elf who has an ugly scar on his face. A smash of Orc Kit's fist later, the elf slumps to the ground, but another Filthy Bastard—a vampire—takes his place.

I aim the gun at the vampire and squeeze the trigger, but nothing happens. I switch to lethal mode and shoot him again—still nothing.

Puck. What gives?

Before I can freak out properly, Kit transforms into a giant and kicks the vampire with all her might. The guy flies to the end of the cul-de-sac and doesn't get up. Exhaling in relief, I switch my gun back to stun mode and put down Felix's dwarf, as well as one of Ariel's elves.

Two vampires wielding wicked-looking knives attack Giant Kit, and a dwarf appears out of nowhere and yanks on my gun-holding wrist. The weapon clanks to the ground. Before I can grab for it, the dwarf throws a punch at my stomach.

I jump back, softening the impact of the blow. Still, my breath whooshes out of my lungs. Pucking puck. Dwarves are incredibly strong, and fierce fighters on top of that. Even with my martial arts training, I'm in big trouble without that gun.

Deciding to play dirty, I dodge the next punch, grab the dwarf by his bushy beard, and give it a vicious tug. My opponent's pained cry is my reward—well, that and the gross souvenir that looks like something a lion might cough up after giving the whole pride a tongue bath.

Hurling the disgusting clump of hair back at its owner, I smash my fist into his solar plexus.

It's like a rock, and there's no sign of pain from the dwarf.

A booted foot tries to sweep me. I jump over it, land like a cat, and kick my attacker in the crotch.

The dwarf barely blinks.

Double puck. This must be a female dwarf—no way would a male be able to keep fighting after that. Both male and female dwarves have beards, though some females opt to get rid of theirs with nano hair removal, probably so that other Cognizant don't make the same mistake I just did.

Yep. Now that I'm looking for it, I see a hint of breasts under her baggy clothes. Feeling better about ripping out that beard—it's often a source of male dwarves' pride—I hit her in the face.

The dwarf staggers back for a moment. Then, with a roar, she launches at me like a rabid honey badger.

CHAPTER FOURTEEN

USING a maneuver from a dream of an Aikido master on Earth, I use the dwarf's momentum to put her on the pavement. Then I break with Aikido philosophy and gracelessly kick my opponent in the head until she stays down.

I don't get to enjoy my victory for long. As I look up, I see a vampire whooshing my way.

This is it. I'm completely screwed now.

"That's enough," Felix's voice booms through the cul-de-sac, no doubt boosted by his suit.

Startled, the vampire halts, as does everyone else.

Neo Golem's chest opens up. In the place where Felix's nipples would be, two giant guns show up and fire at an empty spot nearby.

Boom. The explosion vibrates everyone's inner organs.

The robot points the guns at the still-standing Filthy Bastards. "Do I make myself clear?"

A few angry nods.

His faceplate turns from orc to orc. "Which one of you is Vas?"

"Inside," the vampire nearest me hisses.

"Stay here," I tell Felix. "I'll go look for him."

The metal head of the robot nods, and I slip inside the abandoned store.

The gang has transformed the place into a hybrid between a gym and a casino. There are weights everywhere and a boxing ring in the middle of the room, but also card tables and even a small track, likely for illegal races with small animals.

Sleeping bodies are everywhere. The problem is, there are five orcs.

I dig through the pockets of the first one for ID.

Not my guy.

I check the next one. Nope.

On the third orc, I hit pay dirt. Not only is this Vas, but he's in REM sleep to boot.

Reaching out, I make the connection and get back to the waking world. Then I make connections with a few more members of the gang—in case running around Vas's dreams doesn't yield gnome grandfather fruit.

Leaving the store, I nod at my friends as I sterilize my hands.

"You killed him?" the nearest orc booms.

"No. I just needed to see what he looks like," I lie. "Now that I have, we'll go."

"If we let you," the orc growls.

The guns in Felix's chest point in his direction, and the orc steps back.

A vampire blurs into the store, then comes out just as quickly.

"Vas is alive," he reports. "So is everyone else."

"And they will stay that way if you don't puck with us," I say.

The Bastards step out of our way.

I pick up my gun and stand shoulder to shoulder with my friends as we back out of the cul-de-sac. Once we're out of sight, we break into a run and grab a car a few blocks away.

"That was intense," Kit says, turning into several gang members in quick succession.

Ariel looks at Felix's chest. "I thought you only had one round in those boob guns of yours."

Felix raises the faceplate and grins. "The Filthy Bastards didn't know that."

Itzel turns to me, her eyes shining with hope. "Did you find out where my grandfather is?"

"About to." I touch Pom's fur.

———

APPEARING IN THE DREAM PALACE, I update Pom on the goings-on as I look for Vas in the tower of sleepers.

"Whew," I say when I find my green quarry. "The other gang members haven't woken him up yet."

Pom flies up to the orc and looks him over with

distrust. "You should still hurry. If you don't mind, I'll join you."

I agree, and Pom perches on my shoulder. I can't resist taking on the visage of a pirate before I make both of us invisible and jump into the orc's dream.

———

THE ROOM where the dream is taking place is familiar. It's the Filthy Bastards' abandoned store hangout. Vas and another orc are wearing gloves and standing in the boxing ring.

The dream is a memory, I realize.

I let it play out until Vas goes to the locker room. While his attention is consumed by changing his outfit, I transform the locker room into Cadmael's cluttered room that I saw in VR.

Done changing, Vas looks up and fills out the rest of the information himself, starting with the vape gizmo, which shows up in his mouth.

A few of the gang members are here, looking scorched—probably by lightning balls. Itzel's famous grandfather is also here, lying on the floor in an unconscious heap.

"Call him," Vas says to a vampire nearby, one of the ones who attacked Kit in the cul-de-sac.

The vamp fiddles in his VR for a second, and a hologram appears in the middle of the room.

It's a tall, thin man whose face is obscured by a puck mask, a popular adornment worn at costume parties on Gomorrah, and therefore one that doesn't tell me much about the person hiding behind it.

"Do you have him?" the guy asks in a voice that sounds like creaking floorboards.

Vas gestures at the unconscious gnome.

The masked dude nods approvingly and points at the vampire who started the hologram. "I want *him* to bring the gnome to me."

Puck. It would've been better if he'd asked Vas— that way, I could bring up that meeting in the dream world.

Oh, well. Maybe Vas had met this guy at some point anyway?

As Vas's dreams start to stray away from memory territory, I find opportunities to put the puck-masked man into a variety of environments.

Unfortunately, nothing prompts the dream I seek. The mystery man must've never met Vas outside that hologram conversation.

Giving up, I go back to the waking world for a moment, then recall a few more gang members I'd made connections with and snoop around their dreams next.

No luck.

Outside the hologram conversation, no one seems to have met the masked stranger.

Exiting the last person's dream, I apprise the team on what I've just learned.

Itzel grunts. "We almost got killed for nothing."

"I'm not so sure." Kit transforms into a male

vampire, bares fangs, and looks at me with glamour-ready eyes. "Is this the one who escorted the masked guy?"

I shake my head.

Kit turns into another vampire from the fight. Then another.

"This one," I say when she turns into the vamp from the dream.

"Ah, good." Kit turns back into herself. "One of the more handsome devils. This should be fun."

Everyone stares at her as she pauses dramatically, enjoying the attention. When Itzel appears ready to shoot her with a ball of lightning, Kit says, "My plan is simple. I'm going to take on a different guise and use my feminine wiles to extract the information from that vampire."

Ariel winces, probably thinking of her issues with vampires, and Itzel eyes Kit worriedly. "Are you sure? I love my grandfather, but I don't know if—"

"Don't worry about it." Kit turns herself into a beautiful woman, followed by an even more attractive one. "I plan to enjoy this mission—vampires make great lovers."

"What kind of Cognizant doesn't?" Felix mutters under his breath.

"Technomancers," Kit says without a second of hesitation. "At least so far. Care to prove that wrong?"

Felix reddens, and we all chuckle at his expense. He certainly walked right into that one.

"How long do you think it'll take?" Itzel asks Kit.

Kit turns back into her usual self. "A night, maybe two."

Itzel frowns.

"Fine. One night," Kit says soothingly. "If the carrot approach doesn't work, I'll tie him up under the pretext of more fun and torture the information out of him."

We ride in silence for a few blocks, digesting this even more disturbing part of Kit's plan. Then Ariel and I start to question her about the safety of this, and she reminds us she's on the New York Council and can take care of herself.

Shrugging in defeat, I go into VR and check my messages.

Nothing from Valerian. Did he really give up on me, or is he having trouble locating that werewolf?

For the sake of my mom, I can't accept the former.

I look at Felix. "What are your plans for the night or two while Kit is doing her thing?"

He blinks. "I haven't made any."

"Want to help me with a VR video game? I'll pay for your time."

He grins. "No need. I've always wanted to try it, but I've been typecast as a security expert."

I thank him and ask Kit where she wants to go. After the car drops her off there, we swing by Itzel's place to drop her off and stash Felix's suit before heading to the gate hub building to return to Earth.

———

WHEN WE COME out of JFK, Ariel takes her own cab, and Felix and I go straight to Valerian's office.

"There's a chance we'll get kicked out of the building," I tell Felix once we're in the elevator. "Valerian and I had a little fight, so it all depends on how much of an ass he decides to be about that."

When we approach the front desk, the lady there smiles at me as if I were a celebrity. "Ms. Spade. How can I help?"

"I'm here to see Rattie or Bernie," I say.

She blinks in incomprehension.

"Mr. Bhairava and Mr. Anderson," I clarify.

Felix's unibrow lifts at the second name, as I figured it might—*The Matrix* being his favorite movie and all.

"Mr. Anderson took some personal time to see his daughter," the woman says. "I'll let Mr. Bhairava know you're here. Please take a seat."

Spending time with his daughter? Good for Bernie. He's indeed making progress with resolving his issues.

Felix and I take a seat, but we don't end up waiting long. Rattie arrives in mere minutes and smiles at me in the same way as the front desk lady.

What's up with that?

"Hey, Rattie." I rise to my feet and gesture at my technomancer friend. "This is Felix. He's a brilliant developer. I brought him to help on the *Lucid Dreamer* project."

Rattie shakes Felix's hand. "Mr. Bale mentioned you."

"That's Valerian," I whisper to Felix as Rattie insists

Felix call him by his weird nickname and leads us through the floor.

Looking around, I begin to have an inkling about all the strange looks. The majority of the cubicles are covered by images of me, only with breast augmentations and wearing completely impractical outfits, like a bikini made out of chainmail.

Felix stares at one of the images in a way Maya would not approve. I clear my throat, and he blushes.

"Umm." He clears his throat as well. "Are you a warrior princess in this game?"

"Of course not. I'm a dreamwalker."

Felix cringes. Unlike me, he's under the Mandate, a tool Cognizant use on worlds like this in order to hide their nature from humans. As a result, he wouldn't be able to say he's a technomancer to Rattie without deadly consequences.

Rattie doesn't bat an eye, of course. "I hope you don't mind that," he says, eyeing the images with distaste. "The marketing team is behind these; they anticipate seventy-five percent of the game audience to be men. For what it's worth, when in VR, the player takes your point of view, so they don't really see you much. Not unless they look into a mirror."

"It's fine," I say magnanimously. What I don't add is that I'd let them depict me completely naked and rolling on gigantic breasts as a mode of locomotion if that meant I'd gain enough power to save Mom.

Looking relieved, Rattie herds us into a meeting room, where the screens are already down and his team from India looks at me with the same adoration. Sitting down, he folds his hands on the table like a boarding school student. "How about I give you an update?"

I take a seat opposite him. "That would be great."

"The team has worked almost without sleep since we last met," Rattie says, glancing approvingly at the faces on the screens. "Kind of ironic, given the subject matter of the game."

I nod sympathetically at him and the screens. "I know how crappy sleep deprivation feels. Let me know if Valerian doesn't properly compensate you guys for your hard work."

On the screen, one of the developers goes from happy to worried. "Our compensation is generous. It really is."

"It's true," Rattie says.

I immediately feel like an idiot. "Of course. I wasn't trying to say anyone's ungrateful or anything. Please go on with the update before I stuff more of my feet into my mouth."

Rattie smiles. "The good news is that we got lucky breaks every step of the way, and the level is almost ready." He pauses to give me a chance to beam happily at him. "But before we can let the testers play it, we need to solve a problem that isn't game development, per se. There's a security issue that—"

"Felix can help you," I blurt.

"With security?" Felix looks at me like a puppy

whose squeaky toy was taken away. "I thought I'd get to work on the game."

"I'm sure once you prove yourself with security, the team will find some game-related tasks for you as well." I look at Rattie pointedly.

"Definitely." Rattie examines Felix intently. "If you're experienced with—"

"I am." Felix puffs up like a horny peacock. "Whatever it is, it won't be a problem."

Rattie looks at me dubiously.

"Felix is amazing at his job," I say. "Consider your security issue solved."

"In that case"—Rattie takes out a box, two pieces of paper, and two pens—"let's get to the fun part." He slides the papers in front of each of us. "Sorry about the NDAs. It's a standard precaution for unreleased intellectual property."

Waving his apology away, Felix and I sign the non-disclosure agreements while Rattie opens the box with a flourish and takes out the headset inside. "This is the Illusion Scope."

"Wow," Felix whispers. "So small."

Actually, it's bigger than any Gomorran headset, but for Earth's primitive technology, it's not bad.

"The room is already wired for hand tracking," Rattie says and gives me the gizmo. "It's only right you try it on first."

I walk over to the open part of the room and put on the headset. The dashboard here is basic and only has one icon, a small version of me in a skimpy outfit. When I gesture at the icon, the game starts to load, and as I wait, I read the text under the heading of "Backstory:"

Bailey's mother was kidnapped by an evil dreamwalker, the Rat King. Using her own dreamwalking powers, Bailey finds her way to the Rat King's twisted palace and is about to face him in a fight to—

The game starts, and I'm holding a giant sword.

With no mirrors around, there's really no way to tell if I look like me at this moment. The only parts of me visible are my hands—which, pixelation aside, look close enough to mine. It's a blessing no one bothered to give me those boobs as per the marketing department —they'd be blocking my downward view completely, not to mention smacking me in the face if I needed to run.

I wave the sword a few times and begin studying the dark cavern when a disturbing monster jumps down from the ceiling.

He/it has the body of a spider but the head of a clown. In case that wasn't terrifying enough, the lower portion of the clown's face is covered by a surgeon's mask and the front legs are holding scalpels.

Before I so much as blink, the thing leaps at me.

CHAPTER FIFTEEN

I SWIPE WITH MY SWORD, cutting off one of the scalpel-wielding legs. The clown's eyes shoot fire at me. I tilt to the side, dodging the projectile.

I've got to hand it to the cameras and the primitive headset: My real-world motions are copied pretty well in VR.

Just to see how well the physics work, I hurl my sword at the creature's head. It flies in a very realistic arc and slices at the mask. The mask falls, revealing a clown face that seems vaguely familiar underneath all that white makeup.

Did they model it on a celebrity?

The creature yelps in anger, and a little cloud appears above me. Above it, a text box proclaims, "DREAM POWER."

I activate the cloud, and a new sword grows inside my hand, but it's too late.

The monster's head rushes toward me, and its fangs rip into my chest.

The world around me grows red, but for one line of black text hovering gravely in the air.

GAME OVER.

"So cool." I take the headset off and hand it to Felix. "You've got to check it out."

Rattie beams at me. "I'm so glad you like it."

Felix puts on the headset. A minute later, he shouts obscenities and jerks it off his head. "I hope you don't let little kids play that," he says, his breathing uneven. "Or people with arachnophobia, coulrophobia, and whatever the phobia of medical staff is called."

Rattie nods. "The industry consensus is that little kids shouldn't play VR at all. As to adults with phobias, they can always stop playing when they see something they dislike."

As he speaks, I realize why the monster's face looked familiar.

It shares features with Rattie himself.

Then another thing dawns on me: The villain mentioned in that backstory was called the *Rat* King.

I catch Rattie's gaze. "Did your team use your likeness in the game?"

Everyone on his team chuckles, and he smiles shyly. "My team likes to put Easter eggs like that into all our games. That way, people on the street might think me a dreamwalker and see my face in their nightmares for years to come."

"If you're sick of your face being in all these games,

you can use mine," Felix says hopefully.

I grin. "I don't think we want to scare the user base *that* much."

Felix groans. "Second time I walk into something today." He looks at Rattie. "Tell me about the security issue you need solved."

Rattie explains it to Felix and looks excited when it becomes clear that Felix understands what he's talking about.

I yawn. Cryptography and sleep debt don't mix well.

After what feels like days of mind-numbing tech talk, Rattie pulls out a laptop with proper access, and Felix begins typing away on it.

I suppress another yawn. "What can I do to help?"

Rattie glances at his team. "You can't do much for the demo at this point, but we could use your help with level design beyond that. Valerian said you'd be good at it."

I'm sure Valerian's praise predated the kiss fiasco. I doubt he'd say nice things about me *now*.

Banishing anything kiss-related from my mind, I describe some good dream-world-like levels for the team, relying in part on my game design background and much more on the actual dreamwalking experience. Rattie particularly likes it when I describe the ceiling in my dream palace—a mosaic depicting an archery target-like mandala made out of multicolored glass.

Just as I'm about to yawn out loud again, Rattie

says, "That's more than enough to get us started."

"Good." I rub my eyes. "If you guys don't need me for the next few hours, I'd like to use a sleeping pod."

Rattie smiles wryly. "Of course. The one you last used can be officially yours."

I walk over to Felix to make sure he's okay with my slacking off, and he gestures his dismissal without looking up from the screen.

"Take the nappy nap. I should finish with this in a few hours."

Sweet.

I drag my sleep-heavy feet to the pod and pass out.

———

I WAKE up refreshed and with no clue how much time has passed.

Heading to the bathroom, I see that the floor is empty. When I come out, I hurry over to the front desk. The receptionist is gone too. Must not be regular business hours anymore.

Rattie meets me by the elevators. "Ah, good, you woke up. Felix left some time ago, said to reach out to your friend Itzel when you need him."

"Right." I smile. "Did Felix finish what he started?"

"He did," Rattie says admiringly. "Thanks to him, the demo is going to the testers in mere hours. The rest of the team are now taking a well-deserved break and will resume the development after."

"That's great." I press the button to summon the

elevator. "You should rest too."

He sighs. "I will. First, I need to get confirmation that the demo is in the hands of the testers."

"Good luck," I say, entering the elevator. "See you later."

As I ride down, I allow myself to get excited. Even if Valerian plans to pull out of our arrangement, it sounds like the demo is still happening—unless he shows up last minute and cancels that, which I doubt. And since Valerian said I should get a power boost just from the testers, it's possible that'll be enough to save Mom.

———

THE RIDE to JFK and the trip from there to Gomorrah are uneventful. I take a car to my apartment, hygieia myself from head to foot, change into clean clothes, and eat.

Refreshed and revived, I check my messages.

Nothing from Valerian.

I look at the clock. He's had the rest of the previous night and almost a whole day after that to look for the werewolf. I bet he's located his quarry and has dealt with him without me.

It's time to accept the unpleasant reality.

Valerian is not talking to me anymore.

Just in case I'm wrong, I set my inbox to give an alert if he does message me. Then, trying not to give in to the strange malaise gripping me at the thought of never seeing him again, I scroll through the recent messages until I find one from Itzel.

She says we're all to gather at Nebulabucks at nine p.m.

I look at the dusk outside and check the clock.

If I hurry, I'll make the meeting.

———

WALKING into Nebulabucks is like déjà vu. Felix, Ariel, Itzel, and Kit are sitting at the same table, hot drinks in everyone's hands.

Just like the last time, Felix hands me my favorite nebula flower tea.

"Thank you for your help today," I tell him, enjoying the fruity notes as I take a sip. "The demo is going to be out any moment."

He swells with pride. "It was my pleasure. In fact, Rattie already let me work on the physics in one of the—"

"I think we should let Kit give an update," Itzel interrupts. "So far, all I know is that she's failed."

"It's not my fault." Kit turns into the vampire she left to question. "I don't think he knew anything. You can't fail to extract information that isn't there."

Ariel raises a perfect eyebrow. "Are you sure your wiles are as irresistible as you think?"

"And your torture methods," Felix adds, turning noticeably pale.

Kit turns back into herself. "I was *exceedingly*

persuasive."

"How about *I* question him?" Itzel says, her hand tightening on her cup. "I'm more motivated than you are."

"There's a slight problem with that." Kit avoids everyone's gazes. "I might've... kind of killed him."

I narrow my eyes. "You what?"

She examines her fingernail. "He wouldn't tell me what I needed to know, so I might've escalated the questioning a bit. He must've been freshly turned— most vampires I usually deal with are made of sturdier stuff."

I shake my head and focus on my tea.

Itzel's shoulders droop. "What now?"

I scratch my chin. "Maybe Felix could hack the stores that sell those puck masks?"

Felix frowns. "Gomorran security is—"

An alarm blares in my comms.

"One sec," I tell everyone and activate the VR dashboard.

There's a message from Valerian in my inbox:

Come to my house as soon as you can.

Releasing a breath that I didn't realize I was holding, I grin like a loon.

"Valerian?" Ariel asks with a knowing smile.

"The one and only." I look at Itzel apologetically. "I have to run. He and I have a deal where—"

"It's fine." Itzel waves her small hand. "We'll give your hacking idea a go, with Felix or someone else at the helm."

"Right." I leap to my feet. "Keep me posted."

———

AS I RIDE to Valerian's place, variations of one thought loop in my mind, over and over.

He isn't ignoring me.

The question is whether he's dealing with me as a necessary evil to get the information he wants, or he's actually okay with that travesty of a kiss.

I ponder this the whole way to his penthouse, but when he actually opens the door, my mind goes completely blank.

It must be the "absence makes the heart grow fonder" effect in action because he looks more mouthwateringly hot than I remember—and I have memories I can masturbate to for a year.

"Please come in." He gestures in the direction of the pond.

I walk in on unsteady legs and plop into the lotus pose by the pond.

He crouches next to me, eyes level with mine. "First, I want to talk about the other day."

I swallow so loudly they probably hear it on the floor below us. Is he about to tell me he wants to pretend it never happened? Or—

"I'm sorry," he says softly. "I misread the situation. I thought you—"

"You didn't," I blurt.

"I didn't?" He tilts his head, perplexed. "I thought

you wanted to kiss me, but when I tried, you didn't like it."

My face burns. "I *did* want you to kiss me. I still kind of do. And I didn't dislike—"

"You pulled away." His jaw flexes.

I bite my lip. "Wanting and liking wasn't enough, it seems. I guess I wasn't quite ready yet. I… have some issues when it comes to intimacy."

His face darkens, and his power makes the room around us thunderous and gloomy, like a storm is about to hit. "Did someone do something to you?" he asks with soft menace.

"No, no, it's not that." Recalling the blank spots when it comes to my childhood, I add, "At least not that I know of. I pulled away for a completely different reason."

The room goes back to normal as his expression changes to one of curiosity. "Oh?"

"If I tell you, you'll think I'm weird."

A hint of a smile touches the corners of his eyes. "That implies I don't already think you're weird."

"Forget it." I start to untangle my legs from the lotus pose.

"I never said weird was bad." The smile moves down to his lips. "Please, tell me."

My shoulders hunch. "I've… never done that before."

His eyes widen, the smile disappearing. "You've never kissed anyone?"

"Nor done anything else," I say, Pom turning beet

red on my wrist. "Even if it weren't for my other issue, kissing—or doing anything for the first time—is kind of a big deal."

He rubs the dimple on his chin. "Other issue?"

I take in a deep breath. "I don't like germs."

"Germs?"

"Bacteria, viruses, yeasts. Just name a microscopic creature, and I'm going to be afraid to catch it."

"And you think I—"

"I'm not saying your germs are worse than those of any other person," I say quickly. "Or that my fears are one-hundred-percent rational. Though if you read about the microbiome, it *is* permanently altered with—"

He lifts his hand, stopping me mid-word. "You have the right to feel any way you choose. You also have the right to do or not do things with me." His face darkens again. "Or anyone else."

"If I *were* to do things with someone, it would be you." This time, Pom turns pink, and I hide the treacherous fur in case Valerian somehow guesses what it means.

He gives me a look of pure male satisfaction. "What if the risk of germs didn't exist at all?" As he speaks, the living room around us turns into a bedroom I've seen via his illusions before, one with a giant bed covered by silk sheets and rose petals.

A second Valerian is sitting on the edge of the bed—this one only wearing a fig leaf over his groin.

I blink rapidly as I take in the illusory Valerian.

Somewhere in the distance, I can hear the sound of my ovaries screaming in joy.

"Come to me," Illusion Valerian orders gruffly and stands up, giving me a better look at his rippling muscles.

I leap to my feet as he closes the distance between us.

"No germs," the real Valerian murmurs.

I reach out and touch the naked Illusion Valerian. His chest feels real—and good enough to lick. My gaze shifts between him and the real Valerian. What's the proper etiquette for this sort of situation?

"Before we do anything," I say hesitantly, "you should know I'm not a *typical* virgin."

Both Valerians arch their eyebrows.

"I've done things in the dream world. I've even kissed you—well, a version of you—there before. So I have some idea of what to expect."

"No, you don't." Illusion Valerian frames my face with his big hands and kisses me.

Holy hormones. He's right. This is infinitely better than when I kissed "him" in my dream—and this isn't even real either.

His tongue tentatively explores my mouth, sending waves of heat throughout my body as his hands stroke down my back. I feel like time stops, like there's nothing outside the physical sensations, and knowing that this is an illusion allows me to enjoy the pleasure without fear—and get the closest to orgasm I've ever been around another person.

Panting, I slide my hands down his muscled back to grab the firm globes of his ass, but before I can reach my destination, Illusion Valerian disappears.

"Hey!" I look at the still-crouching real version of him. "What gives?"

"I didn't want to overwhelm you." He pats the place where I was sitting before.

Well, puck.

Getting back on the ground, I take a few calming breaths as I stare at real Valerian's lips. Would they feel the same as the illusion's?

"Was that exposure therapy?" I ask, still breathless.

He frowns. "You mean my lack of clothes?"

"I mean you let me kiss you in a safe space in the hopes of making it easier for me to do it in the real world. I do something like that with my clients—when they have fears, that is."

He smiles. "And how effective is it?"

I dampen my lips. "Very."

"Good." His gaze falls to my mouth. "My illusions are one-way only, so I'm dying to taste you again."

I gulp. On my wrist, Pom's fur turns a shade of pink corals would be jealous of.

Am I ready to try it in the real world again?

I feel like I am. I really want to. But then again, I also wanted it last time—until the very last moment.

"How about now?" I say before I can talk myself out of it. "We could—"

"No." His smile holds a note of mischief. "This time, I'm going to wait until you're good and ready."

Does he mean "ready to beg for it?" Because I'm nearly there.

"Besides." His face turns serious. "We do have important Senate business to discuss."

"Oh, right." The mention of the dangerous Senate case works like the cold shower I sorely needed.

"I'm afraid I have some bad news on that front." He uses his power to make the werewolf he was seeking appear in the room with us. "None of my sources have any idea where to find him. You said you had a guy, so I was hoping you could ask *him*."

"Puck." I rub my eyebrow. "I just used him on behalf of Itzel, and I can't ask him for another favor until I've given him the dream—"

"Please." Valerian's ocean-blue eyes are so intense I feel like I might drown in them. "It's important."

How can I say no to that? Especially after that kiss?

I enable VR to check the time. Napoleon *could* be sleeping. At least he was at this time of night when I did this for him before.

"Give me a few minutes." Turning away, I touch Pom's fur and jump into the dream world.

———

AGAIN, I catch Pom playing sports. This time, he's bowling by himself.

"Bailey!" He turns purple from furry head to fluffy toes. "How are you?"

"About to do something you'll find interesting," I

say, though for the life of me, I can't understand *why*. "I'm going into Napoleon's dreams so he can do his thing."

Pom takes flight and swirls around me excitedly. "We haven't done that in forever."

Because it's weird and creepy, and again, I have no idea why Pom actually likes it.

"Well, I'm doing it now," I say. "Ready?"

He nods, so I teleport us both to the tower of sleepers and look for Napoleon.

Yep. He's there, sleeping like a devil's baby.

Pom lands on my shoulder as I take the guise of a pirate and, without bothering to make myself invisible, enter Napoleon's dreams.

———

AS IT OFTEN HAPPENS IN his dreams, Napoleon is in his human guise—that of a short man with nice white teeth, a slightly curved nose, deep-set gray-blue eyes, and an air of power that's difficult to explain.

Also, as is usual, on his head is a bicorne, while his torso is dressed in a white jacket with a blue overcoat. Underneath the jacket is a red sash.

I look around.

We're on a beach on an island he called Elba the last time I was in his dreams. He must've spent a lot of time on a real island like this because I can tell this stroll on the beach is a memory.

"Hey," I call out when it becomes clear he's not noticing our presence.

Napoleon's head whips around, and he stares at me and Pom uncomprehendingly for a few moments. Then his eyes light up, and he grins predatorily. "This is a dream?" He looks around, the grin widening.

"It is." I make a pink unicorn appear next him, then exchange it for a five-headed cobra. "I need your help, so I figured I'd visit your dreams."

Napoleon's eyes light up with avarice. "Six battles. And obviously, money in the awake world."

"Three." I ignore Pom's excited grip on my shoulder —he wants all six. "And a reasonable sum in the waking world."

"Four." Napoleon crosses his arms over his chest.

"Fine." I make the island around us phase out and get ready to replace it with a terrain of his choosing. "Which ones?"

"Hastings, Bosworth, Gettysburg, and Somme," he rattles out excitedly.

I sigh. "You *know* my Earth military history is close to zero. We've done Hastings once before, but the others don't sound familiar. Except maybe Gettysburg —something to do with a famous address?"

Napoleon shakes his head disapprovingly. "How can you spend so much time on that world and not know these things?"

I shrug. "War is one of the worst things humans do to each other. Why should I learn about it?"

He turns back into his red devil form. "So ignorance is bliss? That's your excuse?"

"I don't need an excuse." I make our surroundings a serene hill where, according to Napoleon, the battle of Hastings took place. "You like battles, and I don't."

"I don't like battles. I win them."

"Sometimes I think you do this just to torment me," I mutter under my breath.

He grins. "I don't, but it's a nice bonus."

Straining my powers, I make thousands of soldiers appear. The uniforms and positions were all provided by Napoleon with nauseating attention to minute details.

Immediately, I feel tired. Aside from blood, gore, and losing faith in humanity, I don't like these war reenactments because they severely drain my power—too many little details to manifest at once.

Making us float above the soon-to-be battlefield, I add a few more details here and there and inform Napoleon that I'm finished.

He frowns. "This time, I want the cavalry to start off there." He points at a spot at the base of the hill.

I sigh and move the soldiers and horses where he wishes.

"This is going to be so cool," Pom exclaims.

I stroke his fur. I guess one redeeming thing about this unpleasant task is that it'll entertain my looft. Maybe I'll feel less guilty about not spending as much time with him as I should.

Turning light orange, Pom asks Napoleon, "Will

you be William the Conqueror or King Harold II this time around?"

"King Harold." Napoleon glances at me as if to say, "See? Some people aren't as ignorant about these things as others."

"Doesn't that mean you'll lose and get shot with an arrow?" Pom flies over to perch on Napoleon's shoulder, and I resist the temptation to call him a traitor.

"Not if I win," Napoleon says with cocky confidence, then looks at me. "Ready?"

I nod, change him to look like Harold, and teleport him to the top of the hill so he can take command of his forces.

Then I strain my powers once more.

All the soldiers come to life, and war cries ring out as two armies face each other. Arrows fly. A shield wall goes up. Horses leap forward. Napoleon/Harold shouts orders at "his" men. Bucketloads of blood are spilled onto the green grass.

Not for the first time, I wonder how this works. Is a part of my subconscious controlling those thousands of soldiers on the battlefield, or is Napoleon helping as well?

Eventually, Harold's forces win.

I turn him back into Napoleon, who looks disturbingly happy—especially for someone whose army has sustained thousands of casualties.

The next three battles consume a lot more time and dream power. First, Napoleon has to describe all the details to me for what feels like days. Then I have to build it all out and animate the soldiers. By the end of it all, I feel like a squeezed lemon that got run over by a bus.

"Thank you." Napoleon squeezes my shoulder—something he knows he's only allowed to do in the dream world. "You kept your end of the bargain, so I'll keep mine."

"Good. Here." I make two copies of the werewolf appear in front of us, one with side burns, one without. "His name is Hans Stubbe. I need his location."

Napoleon rubs his chin. "I know this one. Nasty piece of work. Come see me in the bar—I'll wake up and head over there. I'll tell you where to find him and decide how much to charge you."

"You agreed to keep the cost reasonable."

He grins. "I agreed on four battles." With that, he poofs out of existence, and Pom and I find ourselves back in the tower of sleepers.

"That's what I get for teaching him how to wake himself up," I say to Pom and exit the dream world as well.

———

TURNING TO FACE VALERIAN, I explain that we need to make a trip to my guy's favorite hangout.

"Let's go," he says and ushers me to his private flying car, which gets us there so quickly that we end up sipping drinks until Napoleon arrives.

"Napoleon, this is Valerian," I say. "Valerian, this is Napoleon."

"Pleasure," Valerian says evenly, his expression unreadable.

"If you're who I think you are, the pleasure is all mine," Napoleon says, managing to look even more like a little devil.

I put down my empty mug. "Where's Hans?"

"First things first," Napoleon says and blurts out an enormous sum.

Before I can even start to haggle, Valerian says, "You'll have it."

Puck. I forgot to tell him to never agree to the first number Napoleon names. Hopefully the Senate will let him expense this.

"I'll send Bailey his home address," Napoleon says and gesticulates with his little red hands. "He's there now."

I check my inbox. "Got it."

"You're a useful person to know," Valerian says, extending his hand to Napoleon.

My little red friend shakes the offered hand enthusiastically. "I have a feeling this is the beginning of a beautiful friendship."

Sure, if we redefine "friendship" as "extortion."

"We'd better go," I say.

"Be careful," Napoleon says earnestly. "He's dangerous."

I give him a sharp-edged smile. "Don't worry. We'll live so you can shake us down another day."

———

ONCE WE'RE BACK in the car, I turn to Valerian. "There's something I've been meaning to tell you. Because of their dual nature, werewolves are difficult to dreamwalk in. When I attempted it during the New York Council investigation, I failed."

He cocks his head. "And you're just telling me this now because…?"

I shrug. "There's a technique I know that might help. In the dream, I'd split into two, one of me to tackle the wolf's dream, and the other to handle the man's. I did something like that when I fought Hekima, who, as an illusionist, was also difficult to deal with in the dream world."

His dark eyebrows knit together. "I have to think about this."

I fight the urge to kiss the frown off that face. "What's there to think about?"

"When I make a decision, I'll tell you." He hands me a familiar breathing mask. "For now, it's moot anyway. Like with Erato, we're just going to establish a connection and scram."

"Hopefully not just like with Erato," I mutter and put on the mask.

He covers his face with his mask as well—a pity.

"Remember, don't talk out loud when we're in the building," he says, the mask muffling his voice.

Going into VR, I message him one word: *affirmative*.

He chuckles.

Before I can say or write more, we land on the roof of the werewolf's building.

Our elevator ride is uneventful, and the hallway on the fortieth floor is empty—not that making us invisible would be a problem for Valerian's powers. When we reach the apartment door, I message Valerian to hold on for a few seconds.

I've just remembered the touchless dreamwalking I read about in the journal, and I want to try it again. Not only would it spare me contact with germy skin, but also the need for breaking and entering.

Assuming it works, of course.

I strain.

And strain.

The only thing I have to show for my efforts is a vague feeling. When I focus on it, I find the sensation strange. If I didn't know any better, I'd say a part of me thinks a person is sleeping nearby. Well, obviously people are sleeping nearby; it's night. But this feeling is not just common sense. It's... well, a kind of sense, but so faint that I have to conclude it's all in my head.

Probably just nerves.

I message Valerian that we're a go.

Nodding, he takes out the device he used the last time and waves it over the lock. There's a click, and the door slides out of our way. He takes out his electronics-disabling gizmo and tosses it inside.

Getting his sleep grenade ready, he steps in, and I follow—only to freeze when he does.

Five feet away from the door is a giant dog bed,

where a shaggy werewolf in his animal form is sleeping. At least, I hope he's sleeping. I don't have that much experience when it comes to slumbering wolves.

Suddenly, the werewolf whimpers, and his giant paws swat at something that isn't there.

That settles that. He's sleeping.

Valerian looks at the wolf, then at the grenade in his hand.

I shake my head and quietly crouch next to the beast.

As I touch the fur on his muscular back, I pray canines—and especially werewolves—are in REM sleep when they whimper and flail like that.

With a whiff of ozone, the room darkens around me, and I fall in.

———

I APPEAR in my dream palace—and, thankfully, not in a subdream.

Good. Connection made. Now Valerian and I need to skedaddle.

With a quick wave at Pom, I hop out of the dream world and carefully rise to my feet.

But not carefully enough, it seems.

The werewolf's eyes pop open, staring directly at me.

My adrenaline spikes to toxic levels.

The wolf growls menacingly and tenses for a leap.

CHAPTER SIXTEEN

REACTING ON AUTOPILOT, I grab my gun, aim at the ferocious maw, and shoot.

The werewolf slumps onto his dog bed.

Whew. I cover my chest with my hand. My heart is still threatening to punch a hole in my ribcage.

LEGO letters appear, and they look kind of angry: *You killed him?*

Puck. We did need this guy for information.

But wait.

I check the gun screen and exhale in relief as I show it to Valerian. Luckily for the werewolf, the last time I used the gun, it was in stun mode, and it seems the setting stays the same when you turn on the gun again.

In that case, grab his front paws.

I look at Valerian like he's about to turn into a wolf himself.

He saw us before I made us invisible with my powers. He might tell Icelus.

I go into VR and frantically type out, *So we what? Kidnap him?*

The LEGO text appears even angrier: *We detain him. I'll take him to a Senate facility and wait until he falls asleep again.*

With a sigh, I grab the giant paws. As far as plans go, Valerian's isn't terrible—assuming the werewolf doesn't snap out of his stunned state.

When I mention my concern to Valerian, his reply is: *Just shoot him every few minutes.*

I nod and strain to lift my half of the wolf as Valerian easily lifts his half.

Nope. Too heavy for me.

Grab this paw. Valerian gestures with one of the back ones he's holding. *We'll drag him.*

Dragging works much better. I barely break a sweat by the time we get to the elevator—and we only hit his head on something twice.

Figuring it's as good a time as any, I stun the wolf again.

Once on the roof, we drag our victim to the car and fly toward the city center.

Valerian takes off his mask, but when I reach to do the same, he shakes his head.

I don't want anyone associated with the Senate to see your face.

I nod and shoot the wolf once more.

We fly in a tense silence until the car descends onto a sleek-looking roof.

Shoot him once more and hide the gun, Valerian commands.

I do this, and when we land, I see why.

A vampire dressed in an Enforcer uniform is waiting for us—Valerian must've written ahead. Seeing my mask, the vamp lifts an eyebrow.

If I were him, I'd be more curious about the unconscious wolf.

Before Valerian and I can say anything, the vamp injects our poor victim with something, then hoists him over his shoulder like a sack of flour and strides toward the elevator.

Take my car, Valerian tells me via LEGO text. *I'll get in touch via a regular message. It'll just say, "Ready."*

I bob my head.

As soon as you get that message, go to my place. Don't dreamwalk in the werewolf alone.

Before I can object, he hurries after the vampire.

I tell the car to take me home and close my eyes.

I WAKE up from an intense sensation that's flooding my every cell with warm, pleasant energy.

What the puck? Am I having an aneurism?

My breathing quickens and my nails dig into my palms as an even bigger tsunami of pleasure rushes into my body, making my extremities tingle and my toes curl.

Did someone slip me some vampire blood, or did I just have a spontaneous series of orgasms?

Then I realize what it must be.

The game demo. It probably reached a critical mass of users as I was dozing off, and this is how it feels to get the resulting power boost.

Feeling calmer, I close my eyes and do my best to relax and enjoy it. A few blocks later, the sensations abate and my mind clears further. With a surge of excitement, I process the implications.

This is it. This is what I've been working toward with Valerian's team.

I can finally try waking up Mom.

Unwilling to wait even a second longer, I jump into the dream world and check if she's in the tower of sleepers.

To my intense disappointment, she's not.

I instruct the car to fly to Mom's hospital, then open my VR dashboard and write to Valerian: *I need your help. Can you meet me in my mom's hospital room?*

His reply is almost instant: *Where?*

I tell him the address and which room, and he confirms that he'll see me there.

To distract myself for the rest of the ride, I open up Leal's journal and skim through it. A recent entry piques my interest:

Too much evidence points to one unsettling conclusion: There's an Icelus agent right here in the New York Cognizant community. He or she is clearly placed highly enough to spread rumors that generate fears—and thus nightmares. Youngsters seem to be particularly susceptible, so I wonder if the agent is one of the Heralds.

Wow. Heralds are Earth Cognizant for whom the Mandate restrictions are less stringent, so they can speak about the existence of our kind with Cognizant teens who grow up not knowing what they are.

I look for more info on this but only find a few names of Heralds Leal had cleared using dreamwalking. Seems like he didn't have time to find out who the agent was—these last entries happened right before he was murdered.

A slight jolt brings me back to my immediate surroundings, and I realize the car has just landed on the roof of the hospital.

I sprint to the elevator and take it to Mom's floor.

"I'm visiting my mother," I tell the nurses at the station. "Last time, her vitals went haywire; if that happens again, will you be able to handle it?"

The taller of the nurses, the gargoyle whose dreams I snuck into to check on Mom, says, "Does a mooft shit at the zoo?"

Yuck. Fighting the urge to berate the nurse, I charge ahead to Mom's room.

Just as I'm about to step into the room, I hear an unwelcome voice that's too high for all but bat ears.

"Miss Spade. We need to talk."

I spin around and scowl at the billing administrator —or the Horseshoe Bat, as I've mentally dubbed her. "Do you usually patrol this place at night?" I ask, fighting the urge to take out my gun and use it on her.

Her nose goes up. "If you could step into my office—"

"I paid all the outstanding bills. If you didn't get the payment—"

"There's a new policy when it comes to long-term patients," she says nastily. "We need their stay to be prepaid a month in advance."

"Fine." I bring up VR and send over a payment. "Check your account now."

She looks confused. I guess she'd pegged me as broke.

"Will there be anything else?" I snap. "Any other policy you want to make up just for me?"

She blinks. "I—"

"In that case, I'm going to see my mom."

"The visiting hours are—"

"Do *not* test me."

She must not like what she sees on my face because she steps back and says, "The visiting hours are merely a suggestion."

Yeah. I thought so.

She scurries away, and I finally enter Mom's room.

Immediately, my chest tightens. Mom looks the same, all ashen and still. Even some of the old equipment, like the feeding tube, is back. I have to get her out, but since she's not in REM sleep, I'll have to tackle a subdream first. And if I die there, I'll become a crazed killer, and she'll be my first victim. Which is why I need—

Valerian walks into the room with a concerned

expression on his face. "What's going on? Is everything okay with your mom?"

I nod. "The demo went live. I'm going to get her out."

He looks her over, frowning. "She's not in REM sleep."

I take out my gun, make sure it's still on stun, and toss it to him.

He catches the gun, looking even more confused.

"The password is yitten," I say.

He looks at the gun, then at me. "What?"

"If I don't say the word 'yitten' when I come out of the trance, stun me and get help."

Before he can argue, I grab hold of Mom's delicate wrist and dive in.

CHAPTER SEVENTEEN

THE SURFACE of the black ocean is serene under my feet. Then a shadow blots out a chunk of the fiery skies. It's a flying creature reminiscent of a turkey vulture, only covered in mucus and brimming with pustules and claws.

A bracelet on my wrist elongates into an eight-foot-long furry spear with a sharp fang-like tip.

The vulture screeches something. An odd intuition tells me it's doing its best to say something that to normal ears would sound like, "The master hates you!"

The vulture dives.

I thrust my spear out.

A claw pierces my shoulder, causing searing pain. I instantly feel faint, but I fight it.

If I pass out, I'll bleed to death.

At least the creature has paid dearly for its bold attack. In the process of getting to me, it shish-kebabbed itself on the spear.

Another wave of dizziness crashes into me. With my remaining strength, I yank the spear out and stab where I hope the thing's heart is.

A guttural screech, and the disgusting vulture expires.

———

I'M in my dream palace, in agony. Exiting my body, I heal it and go right back in.

Ah, that's better.

Pom pops up next to me, his fur pitch black. "That was too close. You almost died."

"But I didn't. And now I'm here, with enough power to save Mom. Hopefully."

The tips of his ears turn orange. "Can I come see?"

"Sure." I teleport us over to the tower of sleepers.

Lying peacefully in her nook, Mom doesn't have all the tubes and therefore isn't as painful to look at.

Pom perches on my shoulder.

I make us invisible and go in.

———

MOM DIPS A BABY version of me in a wash basin.

Puck. I know where this is going, and I forgot to warn Pom about it.

Yep. Mom puts the baby's head under the water and keeps it there.

What is she doing? Pom asks mentally, his feet digging painfully into my shoulder.

I think it's some weird hell she created for herself in her dreams, I reply. *Now be quiet. I need to concentrate.*

Pom stops talking, and I ponder the situation.

First things first. Gathering my power, I give Mom a jolt that's many times stronger than the one I usually use on people who have trouble waking up after therapy.

Mom continues to drown the baby-me, none the wiser.

Puck. What now? Showing myself is a measure of last resort; I don't want to agitate her if I can help it.

Dr. Cipactli's earlier idea comes to me, that of using a nightmare as a way to wake her up. His actual plan—using a drug to have Mom spiral into worse and worse nightmares—was too risky, but with me here, I can do a more controlled version of what he had in mind and terminate it if I don't like where it goes.

Then again, isn't dreaming about killing me a nightmare? She's not waking up from *that.*

Then I recall another thing Dr. Cipactli mentioned. He said his drug shows people a nightmare related to what last happened to them in the waking world—a car accident in Mom's case. He said that would be a nightmare strong enough to wake someone up.

Yeah, that's it. A nightmare based on a memory might well do the trick. The only thing about it is that I feel bad subjecting Mom to such a painful dream.

You may want to go back, I tell Pom.

He stays on my shoulder. I take a deep breath and remind myself that what I'm about to do is for Mom's own good. Thus determined, I wait for her to finish killing the baby version of me, and then I highjack the next nightmare by pitting her against the grown me in our apartment.

It works. The dream already feels like a memory—with her looking sadly at that version of me with her pretty brown eyes.

In a tired voice, Mom says, "Not this again."

"Your symptoms are worsening," my doppelgänger says. "I heard you screaming at night."

Her face turns ashen. "Did you walk into my bedroom?"

The other me glares at her. "No. More importantly, I didn't break my promise. I didn't invade your precious dreams."

She exhales in relief. "I just had a nightmare, that's all."

"About what?" The other me crosses her arms in front of her chest.

"Can't remember," she says dismissively. "Can we talk about something else now?"

"Was it something to do with my father?" Both of us watch her reaction.

Just like on the day this really happened, an emotion flashes in Mom's eyes, but again so fleetingly that I can't be sure I really saw it, let alone figure out what it was.

"How many times do I have to tell you? I don't

remember him," she says. "Nor is it a topic I like to talk about."

"Right. If you don't remember, how do you know you don't want to talk about it?"

She shrugs.

"Fine," the other me says. "Fine. You haven't been eating much, either. And haven't left the house in forever. In fact, this is the first time this week I've seen you in real life." She pointedly looks at the last-generation VR goggles on the end table.

Mom's jaw juts out. "Maybe it's because no one pesters me in VR. I'm the parent, you're the child, remember?"

"Look, Mom. I see your symptoms all the time. If you would just let me into—"

"No!" She beelines for the door, throwing over her shoulder, "Don't suggest that ever again."

"If your symptoms keep worsening, I might not have a choice," the other me yells at her back. "If your life's on the line, I'll break my stupid oath!"

It's painful to see how she freezes and turns to look at that version of me, her expression so full of betrayal I regret those words yet again.

She's been making me swear not to dreamwalk in her for as long as I can remember, yet I'm breaking that promise as we speak.

"You wouldn't," Mom says hollowly, backing up toward the front door. "Please say you wouldn't."

"Fine, but you have to see *someone*," the other me

says. "A conventional shrink, perhaps? Maybe make a friend and talk to them? Or—"

"You don't understand!" Her voice rises. "I've tried everything."

"Not everything." There's a determined expression on the face of the other me that I don't recall making, but I must have—this is still a memory.

With a growl, Mom turns on her heel and storms out, slamming the door behind her.

I pay closer attention now, since I've only guessed at what happened after that fight.

Mom sprints for the elevator. Getting inside, she closes her eyes and leans against the wall, muttering under her breath, "She's going to do it. She's finally going to dreamwalk in me."

Puck. I've never heard her talk to herself like this. Our fight had impacted her even more than I thought.

The elevator stops, and she opens her eyes. "I can't let it happen," she whispers. "I won't." The determined expression on her face mirrors the one I saw on myself a few seconds ago.

What does she mean by that?

As I watch, Mom runs out of the building and heads straight for the highway.

No. She couldn't have meant—

But she did.

When the first self-driving car swerves in time to avoid her, Mom throws herself under the next one, then another, over and over, until she finally creates a situation where a car can't dodge her without killing other people.

As the car slams into her body, throwing her in the air, for a millisecond, Mom's face looks triumphant.

Then she crashes onto the pavement in a broken heap.

CHAPTER EIGHTEEN

I SNAP out of the trance and numbly look around the hospital room, the sound of the beeping machines mixing with the cacophony in my mind.

How did I come to be here? Did the nightmare throw me out of the dream world instead of Mom?

"Bailey?"

I follow the voice and see a worried Valerian pointing a gun at me.

"Yitten," I say dully, and he lowers the gun.

I look back at Mom, the computer that is my brain crashing and rebooting.

"Her heartbeat spiked, setting off the machines," Valerian says. "But she's still—"

The gargoyle nurse rushes in and begins adjusting the machines. When the mad beeping stops, she rounds on us. "Whatever you did, don't do it again until Dr. Xipil is here."

I'm still too overwhelmed to speak.

"We won't," Valerian says. "Thank you."

With a huff, the nurse leaves, and I lean on Mom's bed, my knees wobbly.

"Are you okay?" Valerian asks, his voice seeming to come from a distance.

"It wasn't an accident," I say hollowly as the horrible realization fully filters in.

"What?" Valerian sounds even farther away.

I don't know if I can bear to say it out loud, yet the words emerge anyway, as if pulled by a torturer's pliers. "It was… a suicide." I swallow thickly, staring at Mom's ashen face. "She went out of her way to get hit by that car."

Valerian audibly inhales.

An unbearable pressure builds in my chest, my throat cinching tight. Could I have misunderstood what I saw? Or experienced my own nightmare? No, that doesn't make sense. I know it was a memory.

Mom's memory.

Her face blurs in front of my eyes. "It was my fault. I threatened to dreamwalk in her, and she tried to kill herself to prevent it."

"Bailey." Valerian sounds worried.

I sway on my feet. My stomach churns. The back of my throat burns. My heart is hammering in my chest so hard that if I were the one hooked up to all the machines, the nurses would be barging in.

Mom killed herself because of me.

My ribcage feels like the subdream vulture is clawing inside it. Before today, I'd felt guilty about the fight. I'd thought I had upset Mom, which had made her careless.

How stupid. How naïve of me. I hadn't known the true definition of guilt until now. It threatens to drown me, the pressure so crushing I can barely take a shallow breath. Slowly, I sink onto the bed next to Mom, trying to process everything I saw, to make sense of something so incomprehensible.

She'd tried to kill herself.

Because of me.

Is this why she was killing me in her dreams? Because her subconscious knows I'm to blame for her predicament?

Are those nightmares payback for my forcing her to take her own life?

I must make some type of sound—a hysterical laugh or cry—because I suddenly find myself ensconced on a male lap, with strong arms wrapped around me and the pleasant scent of pine teasing my nostrils. "Shh," Valerian murmurs into my hair. "You didn't know what she'd do. How could you?"

He's right, Pom says in my mind. *You can't blame yourself.*

Figures. The rare time Pom is awake, and he's ganging up on me with Valerian. The vulture in my chest claws harder, and the burning sensation in my throat travels higher, concentrating behind my eyelids. Unbidden, a sob escapes, followed by another, and then I'm full-on bawling, the burning tears running down my face, soaking into Valerian's shirt.

He holds me, letting me cry as he strokes my back, murmuring words of reassurance, of comfort. Pom is in on it too, telling me that none of it is my fault, that it was Mom's decision to do this.

Eventually, my sobs ease, and I feel myself being carried somewhere.

I open my tear-swollen eyes.

Valerian is laying me down in the seat of his flying car, considerately making sure not to touch my naked skin with any cooties. Catching my gaze, he waves his hand, and the car interior disappears, replaced with a soothing green meadow.

Wearily, I close my eyes, but the meadow doesn't go away. He's using his power on me.

Valerian appears on the meadow.

I look away, but he shows up there, and the next place I turn, too.

"For your mother's sake, you need to pull yourself together." His voice seems to come from all over the universe. "Once you recover, you'll use your power to wake her and reassure her you'll never dreamwalk in her under any circumstances again. Problem solved."

Exactly, Pom mentally chimes in. *Focus on fixing this.*

I drag in a shaky breath and open my eyes, wiping at my face with my sleeve.

They're right. I don't deserve this self-pity party. Not when I do have a way to undo the damage I've wrought.

Sniffling, I sit up. When Valerian deems me capable

of dealing with reality, the inside of the flying car shows up again.

"Why did you take me from the hospital?" I ask, looking at him. "Take me back. I want to go back into her dreams."

He strokes my thigh as if I were a looft on his wrist. "I think it would be best to do as the nurse said."

I want to object, insist that he take me back, but I don't. Because he's right. Instead of relying on the nurse, I should've made sure the doctor was there before I attempted to wake Mom. I was so eager to finally wake her I didn't really consider her safety.

Just like when I'd made that threat about dreamwalking.

The guilt swamps me again, and I wallow in it until we land on a roof.

"We're here." Valerian opens the car doors.

I blink, looking around. "You took me to your place?"

"The car flies here when I don't set a destination," he says. "Do you want to go home?"

"No." I climb out of the car on mushy legs. "I don't want to be alone."

He nods approvingly and climbs out behind me. Placing a hand on the small of my back, he herds me into the elevator, then into his apartment.

"Sit," he orders when we get to his fancy-looking kitchen.

I comply as he uses an old-fashioned kettle to brew

an extremely pleasant-smelling tea and places a cup in front of me.

"Want me to hygieia the handle I touched?" He walks over to the fridge, takes two sealed manna packets, and puts one in front of me.

"No, it's fine." I take the cup, the warmth seeping into my chilled fingers.

Valerian sits down at the table across from me. "You can have my bed tonight." Seeing my eyes widen, he adds, "I'll sleep in the guest room."

I mindlessly take a sip of the tea. "I don't think I'll be able to sleep any time soon."

He opens his manna packet. "How can I help?"

I open my packet and devour it as I contemplate the question. "I wish there were something that would make me forget I'm the worst pucking daughter in the world," I finally mutter.

"There could be." His tone is gentle. "I just got a message. The werewolf is asleep."

I finish my food and gulp down the tea. "Good. I'm going in."

He spears me with his intent gaze. "No, you're not. Not alone."

"What do you mean?"

"I'm going into the werewolf's dreams with you," he says. "But only if you're sure you're ready for it."

"I'm ready. I just don't understand." I'm the dreamwalker, not him.

He sighs. "I'll fall sleep. You'll enter my dreams. Then, *together*, we'll deal with Hans the werewolf."

Well, if his goal was to distract me, he's succeeded admirably—only not in the way he thinks. I find the idea of watching him sleep incredibly fascinating. Too fascinating, I'd say.

And that's not all.

Getting access to *his* dreams? He'd refused me that when we first met, but I've been dying to snoop around in there. Hells yes, please. The only thing I'm fuzzy on is how much help he'd be in dealing with the werewolf, but if it means I get those other things, I'll play along.

"Sure," I say, my voice impressively even. "How about you go to sleep now?" *Before you change your mind.*

"Right." He stands up.

"And please, use your own bedroom," I say, recalling his earlier offer—along with the circumstances that prompted it.

The dark vise of guilt squeezes my chest again, but before I can give in to it, Valerian heads out of the kitchen, saying over his shoulder, "Fine. Let's go to my bedroom."

I'm glad his back is to me, so he can't see the coral pink Pom on my wrist. I've been fantasizing about some version of "let's go to my bedroom" for some time now.

I hurry after him, and when I step inside the room in question, I realize I've seen it before.

This is the lush bedroom with the giant bed covered by silk sheets he showed me in a couple of illusions. Only the rose petals are missing.

He takes off his shirt.

I forget how to speak for a second.

Without pause, he takes off the rest of his clothes. And I do mean *all* of his clothes.

I gulp, loudly.

He winks at me, then climbs into the bed and covers himself with a blanket.

Hey, no fair. You can't show me that, then cover it up. I didn't get the chance to properly file away all those hard, perfectly defined muscles in my memory banks. Or touch them. Or lick them.

Who am I kidding? If he let me lick anything, I'd probably chicken out on account of the thousands of different species of bacteria that live on skin.

Valerian's breathing changes.

I creep on over.

Yep. He's now under, but not yet in REM stage. Oh, well. I guess I have to do something not so unpleasant —watch his sleeping face. Those chiseled features are more relaxed than I've ever seen them, and that suits him. He looks like Prince Charming in repose.

Legs growing tired, I sit on the bed and keep watching. And watching. For some reason, I don't get tired of it. I guess I'm one of those creepy people who like to watch someone sleep.

Would it be wrong if I kissed his forehead? Would that wake him up?

The temptation is overwhelming.

Suddenly, I feel the same sensation as I did by the werewolf's door, only stronger.

Could it be?

I lean over him and see his eyes moving rapidly behind the lids.

Interesting. It seems like I'm now able to *feel* someone nearby go into REM sleep.

Useful.

Now an important choice: what part of Valerian do I want to touch? And with what part of myself?

Grinning, I gently pull the blanket down a few inches.

Target acquired.

I reach out and place my palm gently on his chest.

Yummy. Valerian's pectoral muscles are perfectly firm, his skin warm and smooth. I can feel his heart beating, and mine races faster, as if eager to catch up.

Wait, what am I doing?

I need to focus.

Calling on all my willpower, I jump into Valerian's dreams.

CHAPTER NINETEEN

APPEARING in the lobby of my dream palace, I come face to face with a gray-colored Pom, who's looking up at me somberly.

"Guess whose dreams I'm about to walk in?" I say, figuring that will help lift his mood.

The tips of Pom's ears go from gray to a light shade of orange. "Oprah?"

I look at those guileless eyes in confusion. "You mean that nice lady from Earth?"

He nods.

"Why the puck would I dreamwalk in her?"

The orange in the ears reddens. "It was my guess. No need to be mean."

"Sorry." I make Oprah appear next to us, then have her slowly morph into Valerian. "The right answer was Valerian." I resist the urge to snidely add, "You know, the guy I was actually *with* when you were awake."

Pom flies over. "In that case, what are we waiting for?"

Shaking my head, I teleport us to the tower of sleepers and locate Valerian there.

Score. There he is. I half expected to see trauma loop clouds above him—he did mention his parents getting killed—but thankfully, all is clear.

"You mind staying out this time?" I ask Pom, following an intuition.

His ears wiggle. "Okay. But you have to introduce me once he's comfortable in the dream world."

"Deal."

I lean over Valerian, and since there are no cooties here, I give him a not-so-chaste kiss on the lips to enter his dreams.

———

FOR A MOMENT, I think I failed and got jerked out of the dream world because I find myself in Valerian's bedroom.

Then I notice a bunch of discrepancies. One is that both windows leading into the bedroom are black—something to look into later. The other discrepancy is much bigger: There's a second version of me on the bed.

A version Valerian is dreaming about.

A *naked* version who seems to be very bendy and more experienced than I am.

I thank the stars I left Pom out of this; he doesn't need psychological trauma.

Peeling my eyes away from my doppelgänger, I watch Valerian's perfect glutes—which are flexing in action. A part of me wants to use my powers to swap places with the other me; Valerian wouldn't know the difference.

Except we have things we have to do.

I clear my throat.

Valerian stops mid-thrust and looks my way.

"Ah." He makes the naked me go away. "This is a dream."

That was the quickest adjustment to the reality of dreaming I've ever come across.

"Ready to deal with the werewolf?" I ask.

He nods, and without my assistance, he clothes himself.

Second example of his mastery of lucid dreaming. Interesting.

I take his hand—mostly because I want to—and teleport us over to the tower of sleepers.

"What's that?" Valerian stares in fascination at Pom, who lands on my shoulder with a Cheshire cat grin on his face. "A dream manifestation?"

"Not a manifestation. He's real. Sort of. He's my companion." I fluff up the looft's fur. "Pom, meet Valerian."

Pom leaps down and lands at Valerian's feet. Looking the man up and down, he says, "The version you kissed looked just like him."

I redden. "Pom, that was private."

Valerian smirks. "Nice to meet you, Pom."

"What kind of Cognizant are you?" Pom asks.

Valerian uses his power to make our surroundings look like his living room. At least he tries to. I see double: a ghostly version of what he's trying to show me and the tower of sleepers underneath.

The tips of Pom's ears turn purple. "Another dreamwalker?"

"An illusionist." Valerian takes the vision away. "But I'm an experienced lucid dreamer as well." He makes a couple of packets of manna appear in the air before handing one to Pom and another to me.

I taste the treat. Yep. He *is* good at lucid dreaming. So was Hekima, the illusionist behind the New York Council murders. He learned about lucid dreaming because he'd grown up side by side with "my kind" in a mysterious place called Soma.

My heartbeat accelerates.

Could that be where Valerian learned it too? Is that why he got so cagey when I asked him about it?

Pom shovels his manna into his mouth without unwrapping it. After chewing mindfully and swallowing, he says, "Just like the one Bailey made for me when I was trying to understand why everyone in the waking world is so obsessed with eating."

I look at Valerian. "He doesn't need to eat because he gets sustenance from my blood." I make Pom's furry bracelet form temporarily show up on my wrist. "In the waking world, he's a looft."

Valerian examines Pom with even greater curiosity. "You mean like the para—"

"A *symbiont* creature that lives on moofts," I say quickly. The last thing I need is Pom freaking out over the use of the p-word.

Valerian nods sagely, catching on. "That's what I was about to say."

I beam at him. "Exactly."

"And Pom is how you jump into dreams so readily," Valerian says. "Clever."

"Yep." Keeping my tone as casual as I can, I ask, "How did you know?"

Valerian frowns. "A lucky guess."

Right. Sure. Nothing to do with the forbidden topic of Soma.

"The werewolf." Valerian looks around. "He'll show up here when he's in REM sleep?"

"Yes," I say and don't bother adding, "Another very lucky guess?"

"Where would he be?" Valerian examines the sleepers in the nooks around us.

On a hunch, I teleport myself to the floor where the nooks have been empty for a while now.

Yep. "There." I point at the one where Hans showed up, still in wolf form.

Valerian takes the spiral stairs in the middle of the tower, which probably means he can't teleport like I do.

"Do you know how this part works?" I ask when he reaches me.

He smiles. "You touch me and him at the same time, then go in."

More proof he's known some dreamwalkers—and this time, he's inadvertently taught me something I've never tried. Normally, I'd jump into the dream of person A, come back to the tower of sleepers with said person, then jump into the dream of person B.

If this way works, it will be more efficient.

He closes the distance between us and stands in such a way that I can reach him and the wolf with ease.

My heart rate picks up the pace again, my physical awareness of his proximity as intense as it is in the waking world—only here, there are no germs, and I'm fully in control.

I run my tongue over my lips. "So I can touch you anywhere, right?"

His ocean-blue eyes kindle with dark heat as he leans in. "Actually"—his voice deepens—"there's a specific way I'd like you to touch me."

"Pom, sweetie, can you give us some privacy?" I ask, my eyes not leaving those sensual lips just a few inches away. "The thing with the werewolf will be scary anyway."

"Fine," Pom huffs and disappears.

Valerian clasps my hand and places it on the werewolf; then, before I can have a coherent thought, he kisses me.

Wow. It must be the knowledge that he can feel the kiss this time that makes this hotter... because it is.

More than once, I feel like we're beginning to float off the ground—a hazard of the dream world.

After what feels like an hour of bliss, he pulls away. "He might leave REM sleep," he murmurs, gazing down at me with heavy-lidded eyes. "It's important that we go in."

Right. Dreamwalking.

Without letting go of the werewolf's fur, I slide my hand under Valerian's shirt and reluctantly plummet into the wolf's dreams.

———

JUST LIKE THE last werewolf I did this with, this one is having two dreams at the same time—one for each of his natures. I'm not sure what Valerian sees, but from my point of view, the two dreams are juxtaposed, like two hologram flicks.

One dream is like a violent nature show. Hans is in wolf form, ripping a mooft into shreds.

What an asshole. Moofts are protected species that are pretty much extinct—no good werewolf would hunt them, even in their sleep.

In the other dream, Hans the man wearing a mooft mask and is in a meeting room, talking to more masked people.

The interesting thing here is that this feels like a memory.

First things first. I can't deal with two dreams at once.

Just like I did when I fought Hekima, I float out of my body and create a second Bailey, this one with fiery hair. Straining my bodiless self, I will myself to enter both bodies.

Wow. It's easier this time. Much easier. I guess that power boost is a gift that keeps on giving.

Wolf Hans stops eating, raises his bloodied muzzle, and sniffs the air.

Puck. The last time, a werewolf was able to detect me this way.

Luckily, Hans shakes his head and resumes eating.

Valerian appears next to the version of me watching the werewolf.

"I'm making sure he doesn't detect us," he says in a conversational tone.

Right. I almost forgot about Valerian, but he didn't forget to make himself useful.

He gestures at Hans. "Can you make sure he keeps dreaming this for a long time to come?"

I nod and set the dream on a loop.

"Good," Valerian says. "Now can you take me to the more interesting dream?"

So he's only here in the wolf's part of the dream. Interesting.

The me in the conference room dream teleports over to where Valerian and the other me stand.

Looking at my fiery-haired self, I wink.

She/I wink back at me.

The feeling is weird because I'm conscious of both winking and looking at myself doing it.

Then the me who was already here notices a hungry expression on Valerian's face when he looks at each version of me in turn. His purely male thoughts aren't difficult to read: One Bailey is great, two are even better.

Well, if he's a good boy, one day I might use my power to have a sort of threesome with him. It might be fun to enjoy him from different perspectives like this. So fun, in fact, that I feel distinctly warm at the thought.

Suppressing the distracting notion, I leave the fiery-haired me to supervise the wolf's dream and teleport Valerian to the meeting-room dream.

Now that the two-dream juxtaposition isn't confusing things, I get a good look around the room.

Hmm. The masks are all the cheapo crap you can get in any store. All the popular choices at costume parties are represented, from real monsters like drekavacs to fictional creatures like Pac-Man.

One specific mask catches my attention, that of a puck's face.

Could it be?

It is a very common mask.

But it's not just the mask by itself. This man is tall and thin, like the one in the dream of Vas, the orc from the Filthy Bastards gang.

Except that would mean Itzel's grandfather's disappearance is somehow linked to Icelus.

"The High Priest couldn't make it," the guy in the puck mask says in the same creaking-floorboards voice

I heard before, confirming it is indeed the same person. "I'll be the one to head today's gathering." He waits to see if anyone has any objections, then opens a hologram map of Gomorrah and waves his hands around until a huge chunk of the map is colored in red.

Everyone's eyes gleam with fear and curiosity.

"As you've probably surmised, this represents the blast radius," the puck-masked guy says. "For the foreseeable future, you'll want to stay far away from those neighborhoods."

My eyes widen. "Blast radius?" I exclaim so that only Valerian can hear. Millions live in the highlighted area, not to mention the Health District is there too— the location where Mom's hospital resides.

Let's talk after, Valerian tells me via LEGO letters.

"Has the date been set?" the werewolf growls.

The puck-masked guy gives him a cold look. "Only the Grandmaster will have that information. What we don't know can't be tortured out of us."

Everyone at the table nods somberly.

"Speaking of capture and torture." The puck mask takes out an unfamiliar device, presses it to his right finger, and winces as the device beeps. "I've just implanted a delivery system." He extends his other hand and taps his index finger and thumb in a Morse-code-like pattern. "That gesture will activate the system. The medicine is painless. Use it if you're captured."

Valerian and I exchange worried glances.

The puck mask walks around the room, implanting

the devices into everyone's index fingers. Afterward, he spends a while making sure the group remembers the suicidal finger-tapping sequence.

Returning to his seat, he sweeps his gaze over the room. "I know how committed all of you are to our cause, so stating this is unnecessary." His eyes glint darkly. "If you're captured and don't use the precaution you've just received, Phobetor will deal with you personally."

Everyone looks a lot more frightened than they did at the talk of torture, or when a death-dealing device entered their fingers.

Valerian was right. These people really believe in this nightmare deity, to the point where they might actually kill themselves to avoid its wrath. In fact, the mere mention of Phobetor has a profound impact on Hans. In this dream, his shoulders droop, sweat beads on the back of his neck, and he adjusts his shirt collar.

The version of me who's watching the werewolf notices him reacting as well. He stops eating and tucks his tail between his legs.

Puck. I can tell this thing is about to become a nightmare he'll wake up from. Well, not with me around. I change the dream so that there's a knock on the door leading to the meeting room.

Hans looks in that direction—and I instantly feel the dream is no longer a memory, something I expected.

The door opens, revealing a mooft standing there.

As Hans gapes at the benign cow-like creature, I

start to make everyone in the room disappear. Before I get around to the puck mask guy, Hans turns from the mooft, likely to ask his co-conspirators what the hell is going on.

Seeing the puck mask alone, he frowns. "Where's everyone?"

"What are you talking about?" the puck mask asks.

Valerian grabs my elbow. "Use your powers to make our surroundings more generic," he whispers. "We want the dream to merge into the one where the two of them spoke alone."

More proof he knows how dreamwalking works— but I don't have time to challenge him on it, or ask why he can't accomplish the same thing by using his own powers.

Actually, I think I know why he doesn't do it himself—he's probably too busy making the two of us invisible to Hans.

I cover the room in fog and cross my fingers.

Valerian nods at the guy in the puck mask. "Now have the pucker say something about Erato."

I chuckle internally. Pucker is a great nickname for that guy.

Taking over, I have the pucker say, "The dryad filed patents that could expose everything."

Holding my breath, I watch the werewolf's jaw muscles twitch as the room around us transforms.

Valerian and I look around.

"Is this a morgue?" I ask Valerian in a voice only he can hear.

He nods.

Hans curses under his breath. "I'm going to pay that bitch a visit."

"Discretion is paramount," the pucker says, crossing the room to lean over a corpse. "Phobetor is merciless to those who betray us."

This time, the spooky surroundings and mention of Phobetor have an even stronger impact on Hans. He backs away, his elbows pressing into his sides as if he's trying to make his body as small as possible.

His wolf self stops eating again and whimpers.

Before I can rein in the dream once more, I find myself back in the tower of sleepers, Valerian at my side.

We look at the empty bed where the werewolf was a moment ago.

Well, puck.

CHAPTER TWENTY

"HE GOT SO scared by the second mention of Collywobbles he woke up," I say, though the tightness of Valerian's jaw tells me he's already puzzled that out.

"Wake us up," he orders. "I have to tell the Enforcers to pump his cell with sleeping gas again."

Nodding, I jolt him awake and do the same for myself.

Opening my eyes in the bedroom, I watch in stunned fascination as Valerian leaps out of the bed and starts a hologram call with someone.

The Enforcer vampire I saw earlier answers—and he doesn't lift an eyebrow at either Valerian's nude state or my presence.

"Sleeping gas," Valerian barks. "Pump it into the werewolf's room. Now."

The Enforcer walks over to a screen with a bunch of buttons and frowns. "He's already sleeping."

He gestures to the screen in question, and we see

that indeed the werewolf is lying there, as though sleeping.

Or faking.

Or—

"Slice off his right index finger," Valerian orders urgently.

Gruesome, but sure to reveal if the guy is indeed faking.

The vampire moves with the speed of his kind. In a blur, he shows up on the same screen as Hans, curved blade in hand.

Whoosh.

The finger and the werewolf go their separate ways.

The guy doesn't wake up or cry out.

My heart sinks. I suspected this might be the case, but—

The vampire touches the werewolf's throat and looks at the camera. "He's dead."

"Heal him," Valerian says through gritted teeth.

I'm not sure if the vamp heard him or just had the same idea, but he slashes his wrist with the blade and forces some of his blood into the werewolf's mouth.

Nothing happens.

Valerian curses and punches a nearby wall.

The vampire comes back and begins pressing buttons next to the security monitor that shows the inside of the cell.

The security footage rewinds and plays again.

"There," I say when Hans opens his eyes. "That must be the moment he woke up."

What Hans does next isn't a surprise. He looks around the cell, realizes he's been captured and kept under. Then his index finger and thumb tap out a familiar code. As soon as he finishes the sequence, his body slumps—but not in sleep.

Valerian curses again. "How soon can you get a healer there? Or a doctor?"

"Not soon enough to make any difference," the vamp says.

"I'll call back." With an angry gesture, Valerian ends the call.

As he grabs some clothes, I try to get my thoughts in order. "What did the pucker mean by 'blast radius?'" I ask, doing my best to keep my eyes off Valerian's rapidly disappearing nakedness. It's too distracting, and I need to focus. "Did you have any reason to think Icelus would blow up half of Gomorrah?"

Valerian pulls a shirt on over his head, covering his mouthwatering abs. "No. Just that they were going to do *something*."

"My mom is within the blast radius," I say. "I need to move her."

He gestures in his VR. "I just made the arrangements," he says after a minute. "She'll be moved to one of the few hospitals not in the Health District."

I let out a relieved breath. "Thank you." Everything's happening so fast I haven't had a chance to properly freak out, and now I won't have to. Except... "What about everyone else? Will there be an evacuation?"

"That's up to the Senate," Valerian says. "But I

doubt it."

"Why not?"

"If Icelus learn about the evacuation, they'll set off the bomb, or whatever it is, right away. Or they'll move it and kill even more people." Grimly, he adds, "Not to mention, the panic such an evac would create would serve Icelus's purposes just as much as an explosion would. Maybe more."

I swallow. "Because fear causes nightmares?"

He nods. "Also, if Icelus are smart, they'll change the plan as soon as they learn Hans has disappeared."

"Meaning Mom won't be safe even at the new hospital?" My stomach tightens with the freakout I thought I'd avoided.

"No one's safe." Valerian's jaw flexes. "Not unless we do something."

To my shame, I fleetingly contemplate getting Mom through one of the gates—and staying off world with her. But such a journey would be risky in her condition. Not to mention, I wouldn't *really* let millions die. However… "What about an evacuation to the Otherlands?" I suggest.

"The hub is in the blast radius," Valerian says. "Also, there's no practical way to get millions through a handful of gates quickly enough."

I blow out a frustrated breath.

"It's not the worst idea, though," he says. "You can go to Earth. Sit this out."

"No," I say with a determination I don't feel. "I'm going to stay, and we'll prevent this thing."

He studies me intently. "You have an idea?"

"Sort of. I didn't get a chance to tell you something. The guy in the puck mask—I've seen him before."

I proceed to tell him about the search for Itzel's grandfather and how it also featured the pucker.

"So we know he met Hans in a morgue, and that he hired Filthy Bastards to kidnap Cadmael," Valerian says thoughtfully. "It's a start."

"Right. And when I last spoke with my friends, Felix was going to see if he could link a purchase of a puck mask to the man."

Valerian looks intrigued. "And did he?"

"I don't know, but there's a way to find out. Give me a minute."

Since Valerian now knows about Pom, I openly touch the furry creature on my wrist and fall into the dream world.

———

"YOU'RE BACK," Pom says. "How did that werewolf dreamwalking go?"

Usually, I wouldn't worry him, but I can't help rattling out the situation as I seek Felix. As my symbiont who can no longer be removed from me, Pom is exposed to all the same risks as I am.

"I'm sorry about that," I tell him.

"Don't be." Turning a brave teal hue, Pom raises his chin. "I'm glad to be your symbiont."

Smiling faintly, I fluff his fur and jump into Felix's

dream.

———

FELIX IS BUYING Maya an ice cream cone.

I make her disappear, and he looks around in confusion.

"This is a dream," I say.

Pom lands on his shoulder. "Hi, Felix."

Felix looks at Pom, then at me. "I'm never going to get used to this, am I?"

"I'm here to get some important information," I say. "Did you figure out who the guy in the puck mask was?"

Felix regretfully shakes his head. "Too many stores. Too many purchases."

"And no other leads?"

"Afraid not." His unibrow pulls together. "Why do you look so worried all of a sudden?"

I push back my hair, which I haven't bothered making fiery. "Where are you? In the waking world, I mean."

He looks confused for a second, and no wonder. In a dream, it's difficult to recall where you went to sleep. Scrunching his face, he says, "A hotel near Itzel's place on Gomorrah, I think." Looking more certain, he adds, "Kit and Ariel are in the rooms next to me."

"Good. Meet me at Itzel's, and I'll explain everything."

With that, I wake him and terminate the dream.

———

I COME out of the trance to a sense of movement.

What the puck?

I open my eyes.

Holding me in a fireman's carry, Valerian is entering an elevator.

"Hey!" I push on his chest. "What's the deal?"

"Emergency meeting of the Senate." Turning, he presses the button for the rooftop with his elbow.

"I can walk from here," I say and instantly regret it —it feels nice to be held by him.

He sets me on my feet as the elevator stops at the destination, and we dash to the car.

"Can we stop by Itzel's place on the way to the Senate?" I say as we jump in.

"What's the address?"

I tell him and explain that I want to pick up my friends.

"Fine," he says. "But have them wait on the roof."

I call up Itzel, who answers in a sleep-grumpy tone. I can hear the others in the background as well. I quickly tell them to meet me on the roof and hang up.

Valerian must have some illegal turbo mode on the car because it breaks every speed limit on the planet, getting us to Itzel's roof in record time. Itzel, Ariel, Felix (in his robot suit), and Kit are already there, waiting.

Somehow, they all manage to pile in, suit included, and Valerian tells the car to head for the Senate building while I explain the imminent threat to my friends.

They take it surprisingly well, looking only slightly wild-eyed at the idea that a blast might wipe us out at any moment.

"I don't understand," Felix says. "How is Itzel's grandfather connected to this terrorist act?"

Itzel's eyes look squinty. "What was the blast radius again?"

I tell her.

She does something in VR, mumbling under her breath.

"Is she doing math in the middle of all this?" Ariel whispers.

"Maybe she's trying to triangulate where the bomb would need to be located to create that blast radius," Felix says. "That *would* narrow things down a bit, but not enough for anything actionable."

Kit turns into Itzel but without the mask. In Itzel's voice, she says, "I heard gnomes find calculations soothing."

"Hmm," the real Itzel mumbles. "It just might be possible. And if anyone could—" She yelps and give us all a confused look.

Valerian must've done something startling to her with his power to remind her of our existence.

"Did you figure out the link?" he asks her with exaggerated calmness.

"The Vega reactors," she blurts.

"That's the power source on Gomorrah," Felix

whispers loudly to Ariel. "Supplying electricity and such."

"Everyone knows that." Itzel gives Felix a baleful glare, and he shuts up. "Purely in theory," the gnome continues, "that technology could be modified to create a device that would release a surge of energy all at once. The resulting explosion might have the blast radius you described."

I smack myself on the forehead. "Of course. Your grandfather invented the Vega reactors. If anyone could turn them into bombs, it would be him."

Felix's robot hands jam into the armpits of his suit. "But surely those reactors are guarded."

Valerian shakes his head. "If Icelus are smart, they'll make their own reactor from scratch, then use that as the basis for that bomb."

I sure am glad Valerian is on our side; he always seems to know exactly what the bad guys should do.

"Is it hard to make the Vegas reactor thing from scratch?" Ariel asks.

"Vega," Felix corrects.

Itzel gives Felix another glare. "It would usually take a team of engineers, but if a single person could, that would be Gramps. He's done it before."

"Not good." Felix tries to wipe the bead of sweat off his forehead with his gloved hand and nearly gives himself a concussion.

Valerian puts a finger to his lips.

Everyone stops talking.

Valerian messes about in VR for a few seconds, then

looks at us in frustration. "I just heard from the team of Enforcers dispatched to capture the Filthy Bastards. The hope was that someone else in that gang knew something." He gestures at something in his VR. "They didn't."

Kit turns into some of the gang members we fought earlier. "That was fast."

"Sometimes even the Senate can mobilize quickly," Valerian says. "Speaking of—I just sent them your theory. They want me to patch them into the car."

"Do it," I say for everyone.

Valerian gestures, and the car windows turn opaque before becoming screens. A second later, Senate chambers—familiar to me from the media—appear on the screens around us.

"Wow," Felix mutters.

You can say that again. All the Senators are perched on gravity-defying throne-like seats—except for the mere-folk, who float inside specially designed water tanks.

Each Cognizant type that officially lives on Gomorrah is represented, except for rare ones, like centaurs and cockatrices. Also missing are the types not allowed residence—like necromancers and giants—but the rest are there, including orcs, dwarves, and elves.

"We didn't see the point of you coming here in person," says an elf Senator I've seen in the media.

Valerian doesn't look the least bit impressed or

intimidated. "Do you have an update for me?" he asks imperiously.

"The Enforcers are en route," the elf replies. "They'll watch everyone going in and out of every morgue. We also sent out most of the Senate Guard to help."

Valerian's jaw tenses. "Do *not* let them go in without me." His gaze moves from Senator to Senator. "With my illusion power, I can cloak them. Otherwise, we risk the terrorists committing suicide."

"Would that be so bad?" an orc Senator asks.

"There were many people at the meeting, and they mentioned a High Priest—a leader of some sort," Valerian says. "We know nothing about any of these individuals, so unless we get very lucky and they're all there with the puck-masked one, extracting information has to be our top priority."

"Agreed," a dryad Senator says and gestures in the air. "I'm sending you the list of morgues. We looked into the owners, but no one rang any bells."

Valerian nods. "Can you also let me know which morgues already have Enforcer backup waiting for me?"

"Done," the dryad says, gesturing some more.

"Me?" I whisper to Valerian. "Don't you mean 'us?'"

"Later," Valerian whispers back. To the Senate, he says, "Are you keeping the information contained?"

"It's been classified," booms a dwarf Senator. "Only the Enforcers, the Guard, and the Senate know anything. And we're not even evacuating, as you can see."

"Nor are you helping the Enforcers," is what I don't say. I'm willing to bet they will evacuate before regular people get the chance. They're politicians, after all.

Valerian locks eyes with the dwarf. "Just to confirm regarding my compensation…"

"No taxes for life." The dwarf tugs at his beard. "For you and your companies."

"And my colleagues." Valerian nods my way.

"Fine." The dwarf looks like he's swallowed a particularly scaly ri, living up to the frugal stereotype his kind loathes.

"Also, Gomorrah citizenships," Felix blurts. "For those of us who were born elsewhere."

"Done," the elf says. "Let's not waste valuable time on trivialities."

Grunting in approval, Valerian terminates the call and examines something in his VR.

"What did you mean before?" I ask him. "The whole 'me' business."

"No reason for any of you to go with me," he says, only partially paying attention. "My illusionist powers combined with the presence of the Enforcers should be all that's needed."

Itzel's shoulders stiffen. "My grandfather was kidnapped. I'm going."

"And I refuse to miss the fun," Kit says. "So I'm going as well."

"I'm with Itzel," Ariel says.

"And I'm with Ariel," Felix says, though he sounds a lot less enthusiastic.

"Well, *I* could actually be useful," I say. "If something goes awry, I'll drop a sleep grenade and invade the pucker's dreams to learn what we need."

Valerian finally stops what he was doing and pins me with an intent stare. "You won't put yourself into any danger."

"Deal," I say.

"Fine." He tells his car an address—no doubt our first morgue destination.

As our ride whooshes forward, I tug on Valerian's sleeve and whisper, "Did you move Mom?"

Nodding, he gestures around, and LEGO letters show up:

In your inbox is the address of the new hospital. I chose the second place where her gnome doctor does his rounds.

Wow. I could kiss him right now, microbiome or not. Now it should be easier to focus on the task at hand—which apparently consists of nothing less than saving millions.

Ugh. Since when do I do things like this? Did I catch hero tendencies from Felix, Kit, and Ariel? After all, they did once participate in an epic battle to save multiple Otherlands, including Earth. I wonder... if I do save the day, would that help me forgive myself for Mom's—

"Why the long face?" Ariel asks, yanking me out of my musings.

"Feeling guilty," I reply before I can catch myself.

Felix's unibrow dances a complicated jig on his forehead. "What about?"

After a moment of hesitation, I tell them everything: how Mom always asked me never to dreamwalk in her, our fight, and her resulting attempt at suicide.

Everyone digests the info in silence for a few beats, even the usually carefree Kit.

"You're looking at it all wrong," Felix finally says.

I lift an eyebrow.

"Did you ask yourself why?" he says.

I frown. "What do you mean?"

"I think he's wondering why your mother didn't want you to dreamwalk in her *that* badly," Ariel says.

The question hits me like a centaur hoof to the head.

Why indeed? Before, I figured Mom had forbidden me out of privacy concerns, but I don't think she values privacy to the point of killing herself to maintain it.

It's something bigger. It has to be. But what? Is there something Mom doesn't want me to learn in her dream world? Maybe something to do with those black windows I saw there?

Something from the past she's always refused to talk about?

Then again, if it were related to the black windows, she wouldn't remember whatever it is. And, come to think of it, she always claimed not to remember—about my father and so many other things... In any case, can you really fear someone learning something you forgot? I guess it's feasible. If the memory is horrific enough, Mom might know to keep me away, even without recalling the exact reason.

Valerian places a reassuring hand on my shoulder. I look up at him. Speaking of black windows, I almost forgot about the one I saw in his—

"Ready?" he murmurs.

I look out the window and realize I was too preoccupied to notice our landing.

"As ready as I'll ever be," I reply and follow Felix and Ariel out of the car.

A group of Enforcers and one member of the Senate Guard are already waiting for us.

Dressed in all black, the Enforcers are armed with daggers and swords, while the Senate Guard has both a sword and a gun on his hip that's similar to the illegal one that I still have stashed behind my waistband.

I sneak a peek at Ariel to see her reaction.

Like in New York, all Gomorran Enforcers are vampires, their powers a great fit for law enforcement.

To my relief, Ariel is ignoring the vamps, her full attention on the Senate Guard instead.

Of course. The Senate Guard are not vampires. For many reasons, most of them political, they're ubers— the same type of Cognizant as Ariel herself. Meaning that, like Ariel, this Guard could jump on a cover of any Earth fashion magazine and not look out of place —especially if the issue in question featured Navy SEALs.

This impressive specimen must be extra strong and fast to have gotten the highly sought-after post.

Valerian notices me gawking at the uber and scowls.

What's this? Is he actually jealous?

"The morgue is on the top floor," the uber says—and even his voice is pleasant to the ear. Looking at Valerian, he adds, "I was told you'd be in command."

The unspoken part seems to be that the Senate Guard thinks *he* should be in charge, but the stupid politicians pucked everything up as usual.

"Stay close to me," Valerian growls and strides for the elevator.

Ariel, Kit, and even Itzel give the Senate Guard appreciative glances as we follow.

On the ride down, Valerian shares the info the Senate provided about the mortician in charge of the place, such as his name and how much he paid in taxes last year.

I wonder what use that last part is to us.

When we walk in, the morgue looks exactly how they're portrayed in the media on Gomorrah—which is not at all like the ones on Earth. The bodies of the departed are not kept in metal drawers but on tiers of floating-in-the-air slabs. There's no need for refrigeration, as each has been preserved using a special plastination procedure that keeps them from decomposing for many years.

The three options for burial on Gomorrah are, in order of popularity: cremation, going into the ground at the enormous cemetery on the other side of the planet, or getting eaten by a few Cognizant types that are into that sort of thing—which usually means a financial reward for the departed's family.

The chubby mortician hovering over a not-yet-preserved body isn't aware of us.

The Enforcers and the Guard look at Valerian.

"Not him," Valerian says, and the mortician remains none the wiser.

We check the rest of the morgue to see if there's any other staff we can look at, but find none. Retracing our steps, we leave the Enforcers and the Senate Guard to watch the ins-and-outs in this morgue and fly to the next location on the list.

Again, we're met with Enforcers and one of the ubers from the Senate Guard, and again the mortician can't be our culprit—he's a dwarf.

No luck in the next morgue either. Or the one after that.

When we land on the next roof, I recognize one of the Enforcers—he's the guy who was watching Hans the werewolf and chopped off his finger.

"Hi again," the vamp in question says to me.

"Virgil, this is Bailey," Valerian says, giving the Enforcer a disapproving stare.

The rest of the Enforcers, as well as the Senate Guard dude, introduce themselves.

Since I'm not good with names, I only remember Virgil's name and that of the uber—Onassis.

Like before, Ariel pretends the vampires don't exist and stares at Onassis's drool-worthy butt as we make our way to the elevator.

"This mortician's name is Wrakar," Valerian says, reading the info in his VR. Everyone looks at him, and he tells us how much money Wrakar made the prior year and other not-so-useful details.

Reaching the floor the morgue is located on, we confidently walk in.

"Wait," Felix whispers when the first body comes into view. "Those marks on the body weren't there in the other morgues."

He's right. The marks are actually carvings in the flesh that are lit from the inside with some strange energy.

Is this some fancy burial procedure I've never heard of? If the intent was to make the departed look more festive, it's an epic fail. The carvings make the body appear macabre instead.

Spotting the markings, Ariel goes vampire pale. "Not again," she breathes, backing away.

I'm about to ask her what's happening when a bolt of energy hits Virgil and the other Enforcers.

For a second, the vampires look stunned. Then, without a warning, the Enforcer closest to Valerian lashes out with his sword.

By some miracle, Valerian dodges to the left— which puts his face right in the trajectory of another Enforcer's fist.

The impact of knuckles striking bone is audible.

Valerian flies up and crashes to the ground in an unmoving heap.

CHAPTER TWENTY-ONE

NO. Not Valerian.

My heart feels like it's imploding.

I can't lose him like this. He's fine. He has to be.

There's no time to check on him or ponder what the puck has just happened. Maybe the Senate has betrayed us, or maybe the Enforcers are somehow part of Icelus—it doesn't matter. Priority number one is survival and helping Valerian.

I yank out my gun and shoot the Enforcer who punched him.

Nothing happens.

I flip the nonlethal setting to kill mode and shoot again.

Still nothing.

Puck. I guess you can't kill a vampire with this tech.

Onassis must know the same thing. Instead of bothering with the gun, he takes out his sword and slashes at the Enforcer I just tried to shoot.

The Enforcer's head rolls away.

Whew. At least the Senate Guard is on our side.

Another Enforcer attacks Ariel. She stabs him with a knife, and Kit morphs into a cyclops and knocks another Enforcer off his feet before he gets the upper hand. At the same time, Itzel grows a ball of lightning on her palms and hurls it at the chest of the Enforcer who tried to behead Valerian earlier, while Felix lowers the faceplate of his robot suit and punches the Enforcer nearest him.

The one Enforcer not attacking anyone is Virgil, Valerian's acquaintance.

He just stands there frozen, a look of intense concentration on his pale face. Catching my gaze, he grits out, "I'm fighting it as best I can. He's incredibly strong. Stay away from me."

Who's strong? What is Virgil talking about?

"So, this is the illusionist who's been snooping around," says a familiar creaking-floorboards voice.

I whirl on the speaker.

This must be Wrakar, the mortician. And surprise, surprise: he looks just like the mystery man in the puck mask.

The mask is missing now, revealing a thin, leathery face contorted in an ugly grimace. Looking at Valerian's unmoving body, he sneers, "He tried to hide you all, but I can see through the eyes of the vampires." He waves at Virgil. "Not to mention, my lovelies." He raises his hands, and that same multi-colored energy streams from his fingers into the bodies on the slabs.

"I knew it!" Ariel shouts. "A necromancer. Again."

She's fought a necromancer before?

Wait. A necromancer? That explains a lot.

Necromancers can reanimate and control the dead, so hanging out at a morgue would be a natural choice for their kind. I also heard a rumor that necros are not allowed to live on Gomorrah—or most worlds where vampires have power—because they can gain control over vamps.

Sounds like that wasn't a rumor, after all. All the Enforcers except Virgil are under Wrakar's spell—and Virgil might lose his fight for freedom any second.

As I process all this, the bodies on the slabs jump down and face us.

Zombies. Freshly made.

My heart rate goes through the roof.

We're so pucked.

CHAPTER TWENTY-TWO

A ZOMBIE who used to be an elderly elf lady rushes my way.

A surge of anger crowds out my fear. Elves live unfathomably long lives, so for Wrakar to disrespect this ancient woman's body feels like a crime against something holy.

No wonder necromancers aren't allowed on Gomorrah. They're the worst.

Though I don't expect it to work, I aim for the elf lady's sagging bosom and pull the trigger.

Nothing happens. My gun can't kill what is already dead.

Having no idea how strong zombies are, I turn to run.

In the corner of my vision, I see everyone dealing with the new threat.

Onassis dispatches an Enforcer with his sword,

then slices off an arm from a dryad zombie. The dryad keeps coming. He slices off her head. The headless body keeps moving.

Great. Things are officially worse than I thought.

Two Enforcers and four zombies corner Felix. The chest section of the robot opens up, and two giant guns show up and fire at Felix's attackers.

Boom.

In the enclosed space, the explosion is deafening.

Felix's attackers are in pieces, but the other zombies and Enforcers near him all turn his way.

Puck.

The necro must now consider Felix the most dangerous target—he doesn't realize those guns don't have a reload.

Meanwhile, not far from where I stand, Ariel kicks a dwarf zombie, sending him flying into the air like a giant soccer ball. "Kill the necromancer!" she yells, panting. "That's the only way to stop them."

She must be talking to Felix, who's kind of blown his chance to do what she says by already firing those guns.

Onassis must think Ariel is talking to *him*, though. Pulling out his gun, he tries for Wrakar, but the necromancer is hiding behind a wall of bodies, not allowing the Guard good aim.

Onassis shoots blind. Nothing happens. He shoots again. Same result. Before he can fire another shot, an orc zombie punches him in the face.

I lunge to the right, where I think I can still make the shot. As much as the necromancer deserves my gun's current setting, I switch to the nonlethal mode— a dead necromancer can't tell us where the bomb is. Hopefully if he's knocked out, the zombies will stop as well.

I aim.

A gnarled hand grabs my gun by the barrel. It's a zombie of an elderly uber—who looks hot even now, in a silver fox sort of way. With a jerk, the zombie rips the gun from my grasp.

I was wondering if zombies were as strong as the people they're made from, and what the uber does next confirms my suspicion.

With barely an effort, he crushes the gun into little pieces.

Puck.

Gun destroyed, the uber zombie throws a lumbering punch at my head.

I dodge it with ease. Strong or not, this zombie is not as fast as he was when alive.

Using his lack of speed to my advantage, I jump away.

A thin, elderly female gargoyle zombie rushes me.

Dodging her, I also dive under the outreached hands of the cyclops zombie in the way.

An Enforcer nearly chops off my head when I pass him. Then two zombies try to ram into me with their bodies, and I barely avoid them.

Gritting my teeth, I keep dodging and running

around the morgue, feeling like an anorexic elf playing American football with orcs.

When I get a moment of no one trying to end me, I pull out the sleep grenade. My mind spins frantically. Should I do it? In the confined space, all of us would go under, including the necromancer and Valerian—if he's alive. The zombies should stop in that case, but if the necro wakes up first, we'll be worse off than now.

Except there are vampires in play. They don't sleep. Would they become normal Enforcers as soon as the necromancer is under?

That *would* make sense.

In my contemplations, I forget to watch my step—and pay for it dearly. An orc zombie gives me a shove, sending me flying toward Valerian, while the unused grenade slips out of my hand and clanks on the floor.

I land so hard the air vacates my lungs, and a shock of pain reverberates through my entire body.

Stunned, fighting off nausea, I check the battlefield.

Looking increasingly pale, Itzel is shooting lightning balls at the attackers. This is not good. There are only so many times she can use that power before she'll faint.

Felix isn't doing much better. An Enforcer and a zombie are pummeling his broken suit, and he's not responding.

The person doing relatively well is Kit. Now in the form of a giant, she's fending off two orc zombies and four Enforcers.

A shadow covers me, and I look up

An Enforcer sword is swinging down at me.

Well, puck.

The necromancer is about to have a new corpse to raise.

CHAPTER TWENTY-THREE

PAIN EXPLODES in my body as I throw myself to the side, rolling for all I'm worth.

Except I don't roll fast enough. The sword slices through my upper arm, the blade supernova-hot as it parts my flesh.

It takes all my will not to pass out as a wave of nausea crashes into me.

The Enforcer raises the sword again.

A dark patch shimmers in my vision. Before I can make sense of it, Onassis's sword blocks the Enforcer's blade.

Panting, I try to sit up and scoot out of the way of the clashing swords.

My body doesn't cooperate. Must be too damaged.

Fine. Leaving puddles of blood behind me, I crawl. And crawl. And crawl some more. When I can't move another inch, I peek over my shoulder.

The Enforcer headbutts the uber and rips into his throat with sharp vampire fangs.

Onassis staggers back.

"No!" Ariel yells from somewhere nearby.

The vampire thrusts with his sword. There's a sound of breastplate breaking, and Onassis sags to the floor.

Puck. Poor guy.

The Enforcer blurs toward me and raises the sword again.

Only Ariel's already there. Her beautiful face contorted with fury, she beheads him with a sword she must've taken from one of the other vampires.

Blood gushes out of the Enforcer's headless body, spraying my face.

A thousand yucks. Of all the bodily fluids, blood is my least favorite. I can't believe I used to swallow it to stay awake.

Ariel bends to help me up, but a cyclops zombie grabs her by the neck. She spins around and slashes at him, beheading him in one swift move.

The headless cyclops yanks on her sword, ripping it out of her grasp while continuing to choke her.

I grit my teeth. Puck this. I'm not letting Ariel or anyone else die.

I drag my finger through the vampire blood on my face and stick it into my mouth. Fighting my gag reflex, I swallow.

There is no pleasure this time, only the bliss of having my pain go away as my wounds mend in an eyeblink. I'll have to be even more vigilant when it comes to vampire blood addiction going forward, but for now, I have the energy to leap to my feet.

Ariel looks paler than the dead Enforcer at our feet.

Grabbing a sword from the floor, I slice off the cyclops's right arm, then the left.

Freed, Ariel gulps in a breath and grabs a sword, quickly turning the rest of the cyclops zombie into minced meat.

Leaving her to deal with the next zombie, I sprint for the sleep grenade. A reanimated elf lumbers at me, so I chop off his head. A dwarf zombie is next and gets the same treatment. Finally, the grenade is in my hand.

Are things desperate enough for this measure?

I frantically survey the battlefield.

Ariel is bleeding but still fighting off the zombies and Enforcers coming at her. However, Itzel is on the floor, unmoving; she either fainted from too many lightning balls, or was knocked out or killed. Felix's suit looks like a tin can that's been run over by a car, and even Kit looks weary in her giant form.

There's no choice.

I have to act now.

Kit's back is blocking Virgil from my view, but I assume he's still standing where he was.

"Virgil, wake me up," I shout, hoping he can make out my words despite the racket. "And don't kill Wrakar!"

Of course, this assumes a sleeping necromancer will

lose power over vampires—a premise I have no evidence for.

Well, here goes nothing.

Holding my breath, I activate the grenade and toss it in Wrakar's direction.

Wrakar must fall under immediately because the zombies and the Enforcers freeze in weird poses. I guess they're waiting for their puppet master to wake up from his nap.

Not good. If Virgil is standing there frozen, my plan is out the window.

Kit succumbs next, her giant form collapsing with a heavy thud.

I can see Virgil now, and my heart sinks.

He's not frozen like his follow Enforcers, but that doesn't matter. Someone has cuffed his wrists and ankles, so all his moving around is just a test of his bindings, which seem to hold his preternatural strength.

Puck. Who's going to wake me up?

Before I can think of an answer, the gas reaches me, and I drop into slumber.

CHAPTER TWENTY-FOUR

MOM and I are standing face to face near a highway, eyes locked like two gunslingers in an Earth Western.

"I won't let you dreamwalk in me," Mom says determinedly.

I cock my head. "Won't *let* me?"

"Yes," she says, her confidence wavering. "I'll stop you by any means necessary."

"Is that right?"

Mom's fists clench. "I'd sooner die."

I roll my eyes. "You don't think that's overly dramatic?"

"I mean it." She glances at the road, then locks eyes with me again. "I'll jump under the first car that comes my way."

I don't believe her.

She jumps.

I stop breathing.

The car rams into her. She somersaults in the air and lands on her back, broken beyond repair.

No! What have I done? The horror is overwhelming.

Shaking, I back away, hand pressed against my mouth. She's dead. Oh puck, she's dead. I killed her.

No, she killed herself. Because of me.

There's a racket behind me.

I spin around and rub my eyes.

Right there on the sidewalk, a bunch of Enforcers are fighting with Ariel, Felix, Kit, and Valerian.

I want to rush to help them, but I'm frozen in place, still not breathing.

Paralyzed, I watch as the vamps kill my friends one by one. When Valerian exhales his final breath, the building behind the massacre explodes. A giant mushroom cloud leaps into the sky, and the wall of heat spreads outward, decimating the vampires and the bodies of my friends in its path.

My paralysis disappears, and I throw my hands up in a shield—as though that will make a difference to the million degrees Fahrenheit rushing my way.

Wait. Something is missing from my wrist.

The furry bracelet.

Pom.

As soon as I realize this, I know what's happening.

I'm dreaming.

I freeze the explosion in its tracks and whirl around. Mom's broken body is still there, lying on the road, and for some reason, it feels sacrilegious to use my powers to make it go away.

This isn't a dream—not fully, at least. Mom did jump in front of a car. I made her.

She tried to kill herself because of me.

The knowledge hammers at me, stark and brutal, the guilt so heavy that even in the dream world, it makes me sink to my knees. I think some part of me was still in denial before this moment, still hoping that somehow it was all a lie.

"Mom," I whisper, extending my hand toward her corpse. I know that in the waking world, she's in a coma, not dead, but she might as well be.

There's no guarantee that I'll be able to save her, that I'll be able to save anyone. Already, Valerian and my friends might be dead. With my stupid sleep grenade gamble, I probably killed them all—and millions of Gomorrans as well.

"Now that's just stupid," Pom says. "And this is coming from someone who's very familiar with guilt."

I look up at my looft.

Pom's coloring is fluctuating from red to carrot as he jumps into my arms.

I squeeze him so hard I'd probably hurt him if this were the real world.

"I'm sorry," he says, wriggling out of my hold. "I broke two promises at once."

It's true. I've asked him never to appear in my natural dreams because I usually like to enjoy them like a normal person. I've also asked him not to read my thoughts—for obvious reasons.

I give a shaky laugh. "I forgive you. In fact, the next time I have a nightmare as bad as this one, I want you to show up and tell me that I'm dreaming."

"I will." He blinks at me with his big lavender eyes. "Now if only you'd forgive yourself as easily as you forgave me."

I sit back. "You don't understand."

"Don't I?" The tips of his ears turn gray. "That dream was false. You'd never talk to your mom like that."

"So what?" I look at the broken body. "The result was the same."

Pom sighs. "Your mom was a mess. You wanted to help her. Maybe you pushed a little, but you didn't know what would happen. *She* made the choice to jump under that car—end of story."

Rationally, I know he has a point. I *was* just trying to understand why Mom was so depressed and withdrawn, and all I said was, "If your symptoms keep worsening, I might not have a choice."

And I didn't lie. When her life was on the line, I broke my oath—and would again. *Will* do so again, when I'm ready.

I take a deep breath.

This isn't really helping.

No matter what I know rationally, the heavy pressure of guilt refuses to abate.

"Well, it should," Pom says, clearly reading my mind

again. "And by the way, you definitely didn't cause the deaths of your friends." Pom nods at the frozen explosion. "Keep in mind that if the bomb had really blown up in the waking world, we'd both be dead now, and thus not talking."

Oh, puck. My friends. The bomb.

In my self-flagellation, I completely forgot about the real danger we're in.

Pom huffs. "You think?"

"You're right on so many levels." I leap to my feet. "If I'm dreaming, that means I'm in REM sleep and thus it's been around ninety minutes since the gas grenade exploded."

The tips of Pom's ears turn purple as I continue. "If Wrakar had woken up, I'd already be dead. That means he's still sleeping. But, like me, he might be in REM sleep. That means a nightmare could wake him up— and then it's game over for us."

"Exactly." Pom bounces from one furry paw to another. "It's almost like you were trying to kill yourself as a punishment."

Puck. Is he right? Did the guilt make me almost give up?

Well, no more. I'm done wallowing. I may never fully let go of the guilt, but I can't let it paralyze me into inaction. If Mom wants to berate me when she wakes up, she has every right to do so, but I have to stop beating myself up. I can't change the past. All I can do is stop this bomb, wake her up, and ask her to forgive me. And with time, maybe I'll learn to forgive myself as well.

"Yes, much better." Pom is fully purple as he hops into my arms. "Now you're talking."

Shaking my head in exasperation—I wasn't talking, I was thinking—I squish him against my chest and take us to the tower of sleepers. I want to spare a precious second to see if my friends are all right.

Instantly, my relief fades, my chest tightening as I survey the nooks.

They're not here.

Pom's fur darkens. "This *could* mean they just haven't reached their REM sleep cycle."

I set him down. "Right. It's also possible they were already knocked out when the gas hit them—unconscious people don't dream."

Suddenly, Kit shows up in her bed.

I almost scream in relief. Without thinking, I leap into her room and jump into her dream.

Naturally, Kit is dreaming of an orgy.

I make all her partners go away and explain that she's asleep.

"Wake me up," she says. "Then wake yourself so we can finish this."

Grinning, I do so.

CHAPTER TWENTY-FIVE

I WAKE WITH A START.

There's a face above my head. A face of a giant—probably the worst way to wake up.

Seeing me blanch, the giant morphs into Kit.

I sit up. "Free Virgil and secure Wrakar," I say urgently. "Don't wake him, but if he wakes up on his own, chop off his right index finger. He still has the information we need, and we don't want him committing suicide like that werewolf."

Eyes gleaming with bloodthirst, Kit hurries to do as I asked, while I leap to my feet and examine my surroundings.

Finally freed, Virgil looks groggy. I shout some orders at him, and that seems to snap him out of his stupor. Rushing toward what's left of Felix's robot, he begins to dig.

Since Ariel is closest to me, I check her vitals, preparing for the worst.

Whew. She's got a pulse.

I sprint over to Itzel.

Another ton off my shoulders. Though Itzel is in even worse shape than Ariel, she will clearly live.

I turn toward Virgil. He's looming over Felix, who looks like one giant bruise under the wreckage of his suit.

"He's going to make it," the vampire tells me, much to my relief.

And now for the check I dread the most.

Sprinting to where Valerian fell, I feel his pulse.

It's faint, but it's there.

I exhale, my knees weakening from relief. He's going to live. I didn't lose him.

Nor am I going to.

Swiping my finger over the vampire blood that's still on my face, I stick it into Valerian's mouth. I know I warned him against this very thing, but desperate times call for desperate measures. Like me, he can go cold turkey starting today.

His breathing improves instantaneously. A second later, his eyes blink open and widen at the sight of me covered in blood.

"It's not mine," I say quickly as he sits up. "There was a battle. Ariel beheaded a vampire. Promise me you'll never drink their blood after—"

"It's okay," he interrupts, and ripping off a sleeve, he wipes the blood from my face.

"There's no time for this," I mutter, pushing him away. "The others—"

"No blood," the now-awake Ariel barks at Virgil. "I'll heal on my own."

The vampire looks insulted. "I wasn't going to give you any. Enforcers don't break the law."

Good points all around. She shouldn't risk the kind of healing Valerian and I have gotten—not after all the rehab. Virgil is right as well: Giving someone his blood is highly illegal. When used in medicinal settings, vampire blood comes from an anonymous donor, and doctors know how to handle it to minimize addiction.

There's a reason I had to get it from the likes of Napoleon.

I catch Virgil's gaze. "Can you get medical help for them?"

"It's en route," he replies.

Valerian leaps to his feet and looks around. "Where's Wrakar?"

"Sleeping," I say. "Hopefully."

As one, we rush to the back of the morgue.

We find the necromancer on the floor, with Kit standing over him, sword ready for a strike.

"As soon as he's in REM sleep, I'm going in," I whisper to Valerian.

"Be careful," he replies in a low voice. "Yours isn't the only way to get the information we need."

I nod and watch Wrakar's closed eyes for any sign of movement. Then loud voices reach my ears.

It's the emergency workers. They've come to take Ariel, Itzel, and Felix.

"Don't worry. I'm blocking his sense of hearing." Valerian nods at the necromancer.

Interesting. I didn't realize his power worked even on sleeping people.

Valerian walks over to pick up Onassis's gun, then approaches an EMT dwarf and chats with him for a few seconds. When he makes his way back, I see he's also gotten himself a hygieia device.

"What was that about?" I ask, glancing at the medical workers.

Valerian hygieias me from head to toe. "I made sure they'd take Felix and company to the same hospital as your mother. And I told them to put the bills on my tab."

If we were alone, I'd probably kiss him twice—once for the disinfecting and once more for taking care of my friends.

And then maybe a third time for being alive.

And a fourth, just for me.

"Can I at least chop off that finger now?" Kit pipes up.

I round on her. "Don't. That would wake him up."

She frowns. "He hurt my friends. He has to pay."

"And he will pay," Valerian says darkly. "Don't you worry about that."

After that, everyone watches the sleeping Wrakar in sullen silence until I feel that strange sensation again, the feeling of a nearby person going into REM sleep.

I check Wrakar's eyes to be sure.

Yep. He's dreaming.

Taking the hygieia device from Valerian, I clean a spot on the necromancer's wrist and touch it with great reluctance.

A moment of concentration later, I'm in the dream world.

CHAPTER TWENTY-SIX

"WELL?" Pom demands. "How's—"

"Still working on saving Gomorrah," I reply and rush to the tower of sleepers.

Locating the necromancer, I breathe a sigh of relief when I see the lack of clouds over his head; the last thing I want is to deal with a necromancer's trauma loop.

"Will this be scary?" Pom whispers.

I shrug, my gaze not leaving my target. "I'd sit this one out if I were you."

"Okay, I will," Pom says and starts his Cheshire cat disappearing act. When only his mouth is visible, he throws out, "Good luck."

Inhaling a deep breath, I touch Wrakar's wrist and dive in.

MY SURROUNDINGS ARE FAMILIAR—AND make no sense.

Under my feet are the calm waters of an endless black ocean and above me are angry, fiery skies.

This looks just like the place where all the subdreams take place, except it can't be: I double-checked to make sure Wrakar was in REM sleep, and more importantly, when inside subdreams, I never realize that's what's happening.

Why and how would Wrakar be dreaming of this? Did a dreamwalker describe subdreams to him? That would imply other dreamwalkers see the black ocean and fiery skies when they end up in subdreams, and I thought that was just my subconscious at work.

Something else occurs to me, something even stranger.

I don't see Wrakar anywhere.

Odd. Can a dreamer be missing from his own dream?

Looking around, I realize the necromancer isn't completely missing. As I concentrate, I feel a presence.

A presence that's slowly congealing out of nothingness to stand on the ocean in front of me.

When I can make it out, I realize that he—or it— looks nothing like the necromancer, even one distorted by the most nightmarish imagination.

The creature is humanoid but taller than the biggest giant. Even without that size, it would be the most frightening thing I've ever gazed upon—yet paradoxically, I can't explain what scares me about it so much. His face is beautiful, but in a terrible, overwhelming way.

If I had to pinpoint what makes it so, I'd say it's those eyes. They make me think of black holes. Looking into them is like seeing every nightmare I've ever experienced. Like looking under a dark bed as a small child. Like licking the floor in a public bathroom. Like—

"Begone," the creature booms, its melodious voice conjuring my every fear.

An image of my friends dying before reaching the hospital flits through my mind. Then one of Mom never waking up. Then—

"Begone!" the voice repeats, and just like that, I'm kicked out of the dream.

CHAPTER TWENTY-SEVEN

"WHERE'S THE BOMB?" Valerian demands as soon as I come out of the trance.

I shake my head, my heart hammering in my chest as I back away from the necromancer and nearby bump into Virgil.

"What happened?" Valerian growls.

"I don't know." I gulp in a breath. "He took on a scary guise inside his dreams, and somehow that threw me out—but I'm going back in."

Valerian steps in front of me before I can touch Wrakar again. "He's not in REM sleep anymore. I don't want you to risk your sanity—not when there are other ways to make him talk."

Sure enough, that sense of having a sleeper nearby is gone, and the necromancer's eyes are no longer darting about behind his lids.

I take a breath to settle my still-racing pulse. "So how are we going to do this?"

Valerian takes out the gun, switches it to nonlethal mode, and shoots the necro in the head. "Remove the finger," he says to Kit. "Then I need him in my flying car."

Kit smiles grimly and cuts Wrakar's entire hand off at the wrist.

Virgil creates a tourniquet from a sleeve to stop the bleeding and heaves the necromancer over his shoulder like a sack of rotten potatoes. We follow as he carries him to the car, Valerian shooting the necro with the gun every couple of minutes.

Once Wrakar is in the car, Valerian gives Virgil an apologetic look. "You can't come with us."

Right. In the air, far from vampires and corpses, Wrakar will be as good as powerless.

Virgil grudgingly nods.

Kit and I enter the car after Valerian, and we take to the air as I try to understand what happened in the necromancer's dream. I'd never seen anything like it before. He must have a horrible imagination to manifest such a creature.

Just as we clear the clouds, Wrakar moans, then opens his eyes and screams in pain.

"Ah," Kit says nastily. "Someone's finally awake."

"Stay back," Valerian says to us and points his hands at Wrakar.

Previously, his illusions would happen stealthily; he never had to show the arcs of energy like Hekima did. But this time, the energy is on display. He's either putting more illusory power into whatever he's about to do, or he just wants to show off.

Wrakar's screaming grows louder. Instead of pain, there's fear in it now, the kind of fear I felt inside his dream. His body jerks spasmodically, and he claws at himself with his one remaining hand, as if killing something visible only to him.

Whatever Valerian is making him see, it must indeed be horrific.

The scream goes on and on, for what feels like an hour. Finally, Valerian stops the energy flow, and evenly, almost conversationally, says, "Where's the bomb?"

Wrakar shakes his head.

Valerian shoots him with the energy again. The screams and clawing spasms go on for even longer.

"Where's the bomb?" Valerian asks again. "Tell me, and this can all stop."

"Hub building," Wrakar croaks out. "The hundredth floor."

"The hub building is near the center of the blast radius," I say. "He might be telling us the truth."

"It's a good location," Kit says, turning into the necromancer, but with the hand attached. "There's a convenient escape to the Otherlands just an elevator ride away."

Valerian levels a menacing glare at our captive. "Who's guarding the bomb?"

Wrakar doesn't answer.

Valerian repeats the torture illusion.

"Everyone," Wrakar rasps when he finally stops screaming. "I was about to head there myself."

Valerian implements the illusion again, waits for the necromancer to stop screaming, and asks, "When is the bomb set to explode?"

Wrakar glances at the time on the car dashboard and grins maniacally. "Twenty-seven minutes."

My heart sinks.

I'm not sure we can even get to the hub building by then, let alone stop something from happening.

"Car, activate turbo mode," Valerian barks.

Turbo mode? Is that why we were going so fast before?

Valerian shoots more orders at the car, including the address of the building in question. With a jerk, the car dives below the clouds and zooms in the direction of the hub with a speed that presses me down into my seat.

Puck. *Turbo mode* should be called *rocket mode*.

Ignoring Wrakar's pained whimpers, Valerian gets in touch with the Senate in his VR and tells them where to send people. Then he curses up a storm.

"What happened?" I ask.

He gestures to terminate the conversation with the Senate. "The pucking morons don't think they can get anyone there within the allotted time."

Kit rubs her hands together. "Seems like it's up to the three of us to stop the bomb. What fun."

When this is all over, I'll have to give Kit the bad news: She seems to have replaced her sex addiction with a craving for violence. And while we're at it, I'll make her aware of the real definition of the word "fun."

Valerian shoots Wrakar with his mojo again. After he deems the screaming sufficient, he stops the torture and asks, "How do we deactivate the bomb?"

"I don't know," Wrakar croaks. "Only the High Priest knows."

Frowning, Valerian shoots Wrakar with the illusion energy a few more times, but the answer stays the same.

Valerian looks at Kit. "Do you have a way to disable him, temporarily? If we walk into that building and it turns out that he lied, I want him alive to regret it."

Kit looks thoughtful for a second, then grins. "If you don't like spiders, you might want to look away."

I don't know about Valerian, but I jerk my gaze away and put my hands over my ears for good measure.

Even through my palms, I can hear Wrakar yelling in horror. He swears on everything from his mother's remains to his own life that he didn't lie to us, and begs for Kit to stop whatever it is she's doing.

Eventually, Wrakar's vocal cords must give out, because instead of screaming, he just produces a prolonged hoarse croak.

"There," Kit says eventually. "He's not going anywhere."

When I turn, I see what I sort of expected—and it's still extremely disturbing. The necromancer's ghost-pale face is sticking out of a giant silk cocoon of the type spiders use to wrap their prey.

"So," I say, my voice shaky. "What's the plan?"

"We go in," Valerian says. "I make sure they can't see us. When we know which one is the High Priest, we apprehend him while I make sure the others are none the wiser. I then make him tell us how to disable the bomb, and we do just that. Afterward, I can make it so that Icelus kill each other, or maybe we knock them out one by one." He looks at me. "Which do you prefer?"

"Knocking them out is safer," I say. "We don't know what powers they have. They might hurt us in the process of attacking one another."

Nodding, Valerian lands the car smack in the middle of the hub, which I'm pretty sure is illegal. Ignoring the gates all around us, we sprint for the elevator, where I smash the button for the hundredth floor.

A quick ride later, the elevator doors ding open and we exit—straight into a horde of Icelus.

CHAPTER TWENTY-EIGHT

THIS FLOOR IS CLEARLY MEANT to be rented out for big parties, like weddings and Jubilees, but that's not how it's being used at the moment. Far from it.

A row of hospital beds stands where dining tables usually would. On the beds are comatose people who must be sleeping—I know because my newfound REM sleep sense can detect many of them dreaming.

Next to each bed stands an Icelus member. They're all wearing the masks from the werewolf's dream and holding intricately designed daggers, their attention on the podium where the wedding band would typically be.

Following their gazes, I audibly exhale.

A black-clad figure stands with his or her back to us, fiddling with an unfamiliar device.

My heartbeat skyrockets.

It's not that hard to guess what's happening. The figure is the High Priest, and the beeping device is the reactor-turned-bomb. Most concerning, on the screen where the married couple would usually watch a video collage is a digital clock counting down seconds.

Everyone stares at the remaining time.

Ten minutes and ten seconds.

Do you think it's until the explosion? I message Valerian. *Or the moment they should run upstairs if they mean to escape via the gates?*

Let's assume time to explosion, he replies. *I wouldn't put it past these fanatics to blow themselves up for their deity.*

Oh, yeah. I forgot about the deity part. These idiots worship Phobetor—or Collywobbles, as far as Valerian's concerned.

The countdown hits ten minutes exactly.

It must be some critical milestone in whatever's about to happen because the walls all around the room turn into screens displaying a slideshow of horror-movie-worthy images.

Wait a second. I've seen something like this before. It was—

The black-clad High Priest turns from the bomb to face the Icelus members and announces in a booming voice, "The first sacrifice."

A thin elf in a drekavac mask stabs the sleeper nearest him.

My jaw drops open—but not from the violence I've just witnessed.

I know the High Priest, know that Darth Vader-like mask and voice.

It's Doctor Cipactli, the gnome who works at the sleep clinic I nearly put Mom in.

Puck.

She could've been that sacrifice.

Speaking of sacrifices, they now make a macabre kind of sense. The sleepers must be having nightmares, so the Icelus fanatics probably think that killing someone in that state will bring them closer to the nightmare deity, or some nonsense like that.

Cipactli's clinic is where I've seen those subdream-like images, too.

Hold on.

I scan the sleepers.

Yep. Gertrude, the gangrene-giver from the New York Council, is right there. Poor wretch. We're not exactly pals, but I don't want her to be a sacrifice to a made-up god.

Another sleeper, on a bed near Gertrude, catches my eye.

It's Cadmael, Itzel's grandfather.

Focusing my REM sleep radar power on him tells me he's dreaming, so he's alive for now.

I wish Itzel were here so I could reassure her.

Frantically opening my VR, I write everything I've just realized for Valerian, adding that Doctor Cipactli studies nightmares—a natural subject of interest for a worshiper of a deity like Collywobbles.

Valerian pulls out a gun just as LEGO letters show up in front of me, chilling me to the bone: *He's a gnome!?*

Pucking puck. Most powers don't work on gnomes.

Valerian takes aim, but he's hesitating and I can understand why. We need the gnome conscious to tell us how to disable the bomb. The stun of the gun might knock him out for longer than the time we have left. An equally good question is *how* we'd make him talk in the first place. Valerian can't use his illusion torture on a gnome—and even if we magically got the High Priest to sleep, I wouldn't be able to get the answers either; as I recently learned, I would need the gnome's consent.

I glance at the stage.

Crap. The High Priest is looking right at us, a lightning ball already in his hands.

Valerian seems to finally come to a decision, but before he squeezes the trigger, the High Priest launches his projectile.

The ball of energy zooms toward us with the speed of light—and smashes straight into Valerian's chest.

CHAPTER TWENTY-NINE

NO. Not again.

Spinning on my heel, I lunge toward his fallen body.

From behind me, a giant's voice booms, "I'll hold them off!"

That must be Kit. No doubt she's changed to match that voice.

A second later, the sound of her enormous fist slamming into someone's flesh confirms it.

I block out the sounds of the fight, focusing on the prone figure in front of me. Valerian's clothes are singed where the ball hit him, but the skin underneath isn't charred, just reddened, like after a bad sunburn.

The breath I've been holding escapes my lungs. He must know how much of a trouble magnet he is, and wore protective gear.

I check his pulse. Faint but there.

My own pulse settles into a steadier rhythm. Swiftly, I scan myself for any hint of vampire blood from earlier. I know I said he needs to abstain, but I'd rather he live as an addict than not at all.

No blood left. All cleaned up by Valerian himself.

"Crap." Kit's voice sounds tiny this time, as though she's inhaled a bunch of helium.

It jerks me back to what's happening. As much as I want to fuss over Valerian, there's an impossible task before us: stop the bomb before the timer runs out.

I pry the gun out of his fingers.

The gun is dead. The electricity of the High Priest's projectile must've fried something. Holding the useless weapon, I leap to my feet and face Kit.

She's a giant again—and kicking a gargoyle Icelus in a harlequin mask.

The High Priest hurls another lightning ball at Kit.

She turns into something small with wings—either a pixie or a hummingbird.

The projectile whooshes through the empty air.

The elf in a drekavac mask, the one who made the sacrifice earlier, runs under tiny Kit and heads straight for me.

Kit turns back into a giant, preventing any other Icelus from coming this way.

I aim at the elf. "Freeze!" I order in my best imitation of a cop's voice. "Drop the knife, or I'll shoot."

The elf keeps coming, his face unreadable under that mask.

Puck. He's calling my bluff. Gulping in a panicked breath, I wait until he's almost upon me before I hurl the gun at his head.

The elf must've had some training. He dodges the projectile with ease and sneers, "Did you bring a broken gun to a knife fight?"

Crouching, I sweep at his legs. He jumps over my foot and slashes at me with his dagger.

Pain sears through me. The knife has just sliced through my forearm.

I grit my teeth, ignoring both the pain and the panic I feel at the thought of the earlier victim's blood mixing with mine. If I freak out, I'm as good as dead. Even without the freak out, there's probably less than nine minutes left to live.

Hoping it's the last thing he'd expect, I uppercut the elf with my injured arm.

The injury makes my swing clumsy, and the elf jerks his head back before coming at my throat with a dagger.

I catch his wrist before the blade connects.

He goes to punch me, but I catch that wrist as well.

Thank puck he's especially skinny.

He tries to twist out of my grip, but I hold on with all my strength, ignoring the blood spurting from my arm.

Eyes cutting to my injury, he hisses, "How long do you think you can keep this up?"

I headbutt him in reply, my forehead smashing into the drekavac mask. The mask splits. Stars explode in my vision—but hopefully even more in his.

He kicks me in the knee. My kneecap screams in

agony. He jerks on his wrists again and pushes me with his whole body.

I lose balance, taking him with me as I fall.

Ouch. I land on my back, air whooshing out of my lungs. To my shock, I'm still gripping his wrists.

He aims the dagger at my neck and presses down. I let go of his left wrist and grasp his right one with both hands to keep the knife from reaching me. The blood from my forearm drips onto my face, but I ignore it, straining with all I've got.

He grabs the knife with his free hand and pushes harder.

I do my best to hold him, but a male, even a skinny elf, is stronger than me.

Inch by inch, the knife descends.

CHAPTER THIRTY

AN INSANE IDEA occurs to me, and there's no time to figure out if it will work or not.

I unclasp my left hand from his wrist.

Now that it's his two arms against one of mine, the knife descends faster.

I regrasp, putting my left hand around his right.

His teeth audibly grind together. "No way you'll snatch my dagger."

If I had any breath left for trash talk, I'd tell him that I don't need to. Instead, I reach for his index finger with mine and tap out the Morse-code-like pattern I saw in the werewolf's dream.

At least, I hope it's the pattern. Stress could've messed with my memory, or for that matter, they could've already disabled the "don't get taken alive" device.

Behind his cracked mask, the elf's eyes widen—then go blank.

When he slumps, I roll him off me and extract the dagger from his grasp.

Sucking in shallow breaths, I sit up. My head spins, my vision spotty with black. Fighting not to faint, I struggle to my feet and nearly cry out at the pain in my knee.

My legs hold me, but just barely.

According to the countdown clock, we have five minutes left. Even if I knew how to disable the thing, I doubt I'd make it through the Icelus in time.

Then again, there are fewer Icelus alive, thanks to Kit. And another bit of good news is that the High Priest must be tired of generating all that lightning because instead of hurling another ball, he shouts, "Free the sacrifices! Some of them sleepwalk. Might keep that giant busy."

Puck him. It's a good plan. If other sleepers are anything like Gertrude, the last thing we want is for Kit to face them. Though... in their sleepwalking, they're just as likely to hurt the bad guys as they are us.

Hopefully.

A dwarf in a Pac-Man mask rushes to execute his leader's order. One by one he unbinds every sleeper, even Cadmael. Right away, some of them—Gertrude included—rise from the beds and start walking aimlessly.

Itzel's grandfather stays put. Unlike the others, he has no sleep disorders and is just drugged. In fact, I can still feel him in REM sleep.

Limping, I move forward, step after agonizing step.

My vague plan is to somehow make it to that stage and force the High Priest to stop the bomb by holding my knife to his throat.

No idea how I'll make it so he doesn't fry me with his power, or what I'll do if he's willing to die for his beliefs—which is clearly the case.

"Cover me," I say to Kit as I close the distance between us.

In reply, she stomps and punches everyone near her, clearing me a path.

I limp farther.

Kit clears the path again.

We're a sprint away from the stage, only I can't sprint even to save all those millions of lives.

The High Priest must not think me a real threat because the next lightning ball he hurls flies at Kit. She does the turn-to-pixie trick again and remains unscathed.

I clench my teeth and stagger forward—only to realize Gertrude has wandered my way.

Arms flailing in random movements, she's nearly upon me.

CHAPTER THIRTY-ONE

PUCK. All she needs to do is touch me, and whatever body part she gets, I'll lose.

Except she's dreaming, so she can't see me.

Gambling on that, I turn sideways moments before she can brush her fingers over my face. She passes right by. However, if she keeps heading in that direction, she's going to be a problem for Kit.

I recall something from the time I had to sleepwalk in her during my Council investigation.

Touching her *hair* is okay.

Without giving it too much thought, I whack the back of her head with the knife handle. Then, for good measure, I do it again.

As she drops like a stone, I realize this is the second time I've knocked her out under dire circumstances. One more, and the universe should let me punch her out for free.

I turn back to the stage—and come nose to nose

with the High Priest, who promptly aims a kick at my injured knee.

It buckles underneath me, and I fall onto all fours.

Through the haze of pain, I realize this is it.

I've blown my only chance to overpower the gnome.

But hold on. The High Priest isn't the only gnome here who has the information I need. As the inventor of the reactor, Cadmael was the one who'd turned it into a bomb. I bet he can help disable it too. With all the fighting for my life, I didn't get a chance to think of this earlier.

Above me, the High Priest forms another lightning ball and shoots it at Kit.

Kit transforms before getting hit.

I look at the far, far away bed where Cadmael is. If I were there, I'd jump into his dream and wake him up—I can still feel him in REM sleep. But given the state of my leg, I'd have to crawl, which means there's no way I'd make it there in time.

Maybe Kit could throw me. But no, she's too busy with her own battle. Besides, who says I'd land in any condition to dreamwalk? I can barely stay conscious as is.

Then I remember it.

Touchless dreamwalking.

I haven't tried it since the beta testers gave me a boost of power. There's a chance I could make it work now.

Closing my eyes, I extend my hand in the direction of Cadmael's bed and strain to make the connection.

It doesn't work.

I strain harder.

Nope.

I take another route. I imagine standing there, above the elderly gnome's tiny body. I imagine touching his wrinkled forehead, picture how I'd want to clean my hand afterward.

The exercise is effective in that I can almost feel the germy skin under my fingers.

Still, nothing happens.

No, wait.

Something *is* happening.

Something both odd and familiar.

There's a small voice in my head, a voice that seems to be saying, *Who are you, and what do you want?*

Of course. He's a gnome, so I need his consent.

My name is Bailey. I'm a friend of Itzel, your granddaughter. I'm trying to help you. Please let me in.

No mental reply comes, but something yields and I enter the gnome's dream world.

CHAPTER THIRTY-TWO

IGNORING a barrage of questions from Pom, I teleport to the tower of sleepers as soon as I appear in my palace. Swiftly, I find Cadmael and leap into his dream.

A dream that is clearly a nightmare.

Icelus agents are cutting Itzel into small pieces with their ceremonial daggers while Cadmael is tied up and powerless to save his granddaughter.

Not bothering with subtlety, I evaporate Icelus, make Itzel whole, and have her kiss her grandfather on the cheek before sprinting out of the room. Finally, I free the gnome from his nightmare bindings.

He rubs his rope-burned wrists and stares at me with utter incomprehension. "How?"

"You're dreaming," I say calmly. "That was a nightmare. I'm a dreamwalker. My name is Bailey."

"Bailey," he says, still looking stunned. "Itzel mentioned you."

"Great," I say quickly. "Sadly, we don't have time to get better acquainted. Icelus kidnapped you. They made you build a bomb from Vega reactor technology."

He looks like I've slapped him.

Good. I need him to snap out of the dream haze and smell the apocalypse.

"Did it go off?" he asks, his voice small. "How many dead?"

"It hasn't exploded yet, but it could at any moment. Which is why I need you to wake up and disable it."

The gnome's back straightens. "Where is it?"

I turn the room around us into the hundredth floor of the hub building—with Icelus, the bomb, and the rest of it.

"You're here." I point at his bed. "The bomb is there." I point at the podium. "Make sure to avoid him." I point at where the High Priest stands over my body.

Eyeing the High Priest warily, Cadmael nods. "How do I wake up?"

"Just wish to do so," I say.

He closes his eyes.

I help him with a jolt of my power.

He stays, eyes still closed.

Whatever they gave him to make him sleep is strong.

Only I'm stronger. Quadrupling my usual jolt, I shoot Cadmael with it.

It works.

He disappears and I find myself back in the tower

of sleepers, where Pom stares at me with an unblinking gaze.

"We might survive this yet," I tell him and terminate the dream.

CHAPTER THIRTY-THREE

I COME out of the trance to the sound of a lightning ball smashing into a distant wall.

Kit is in pixie form, which is how she's dodged the projectile again.

Sneaking a peek at the beds, I see Cadmael get up.

Yes! Now we just need to keep the High Priest from noticing this development.

Kit spots Cadmael too and reaches the same conclusion. Abandoning her pixie shape, she turns into a drekavac.

Now we're talking. All she needs is to touch the High Priest with one of those pustule-covered tentacles, and the evil gnome will be writhing on the floor in pain.

Realizing the same thing, the High Priest dodges Kit's appendage and sticks his hand into his pocket.

With all my remaining strength, I grasp my knife. Before I can summon enough energy for a stab, the

High Priest notices my intent and jerks his hand out of his pocket.

In his grasp is a vaguely familiar device.

There's a hiss.

I blink in confusion. My knife is in the hands of the High Priest.

Pucking blood loss. It made me miss the moment he took that from me.

Drekavac Kit whips another tentacle at the High Priest.

He slices at it with the dagger.

The tentacle drops to the floor.

Kit's scream is as horrific as her drekavac form's appearance.

Seizing the moment, the High Priest hurls the knife at Kit's head and follows up with a lightning ball.

The blade enters Drekavac Kit's eye. She screams even louder—which is when the lightning ball smashes into her chest.

The drekavac becomes Kit once more, only with a missing hand and a charred hole in the middle of her chest; her clothing wasn't as protective as Valerian's.

The High Priest shoots her with another lightning ball. Then another.

Kit collapses, now a charred corpse.

No. Not Kit. I can't lose—

The High Priest turns to the stage.

Puck. He wasn't supposed to notice Cadmael. But he does—and shoots the older gnome with a ball of lightning.

Cadmael drops to the floor.

Puck, puck, puck.

He was but a few feet away from the bomb. It might as well be thousands of miles now—the digital countdown on the screen reaches zero.

I gasp in horror as the bomb explodes, the wave of heat spreading in a vaguely familiar fashion.

Suddenly, Pom shows up between me and the approaching demise.

His fur is pitch black, his lavender eyes wild. "You said to let you know if you're having a nightmare," he pants. "I'm letting you know."

A nightmare? As in, a dream?

I stop the explosion. Exiting my body, I heal it and jump back in.

Wow. I *am* dreaming. But how? Or the better question is: When did it start?

For a second, I entertain a fantasy that this whole thing, the bomb and Icelus, was a bad dream. But no. Now that the pain isn't clouding my mind, I know exactly what happened.

That device and that hissing sound—I remember them both. When I met the High Priest as Dr. Cipactli, he used this very thing to put himself into REM sleep in order to sample my powers.

Koshmar, he called the drug. He said it creates nightmares that get progressively worse. He also said that the first one always features whatever the sleeper experienced right before falling asleep—in this case, the continuation of our fight.

I float up in relief.

Everything I experienced after that hiss, including Kit's death and the explosion, was a nightmare.

Kit is still alive out in the waking world.

The bomb didn't explode.

Cadmael might still make it.

Maybe. Hopefully.

Regardless, I can't believe Dr. Capactli was offering to use this drug to wake Mom. I'd dodged a huge bullet when I rejected his help. If I'd let Mom be his patient, she'd be in this room as one of the sacrifices.

The bastard. He clearly lied about the most important aspect of this drug. He claimed that if a nightmare gets bad enough, the sleeper wakes up. That's obviously not how it works, else I would've woken up as soon as Kit was killed—and Cadmael when Itzel was tortured. It seems like the real way this Koshmar works is to keep someone in nightmares indefinitely, an evil only a follower of Phobetor would dream up.

I wonder what would've happened to me if I'd accepted his job offer.

Nothing good, I'm sure.

On a hunch, I teleport to the tower of sleepers—specifically into Kit's nook.

It's as I thought.

She's here, dreaming.

"Dr. Cipactli—that is, the High Priest—didn't just spray me," I explain to Pom, who appears beside me. "I need to wake her first."

Grabbing Kit's hand, I jump into her dream.

———

KIT IS in the same cursed room on the hundredth floor —no surprise there. She's watching as the High Priest disembowels me. The me in Kit's dream, that is.

The grief on her face is touching. I didn't realize she cared that much about me.

I freeze the scene, turn the High Priest into a toad, and stand so she can see me.

"What's this?" she asks, eyes rounding.

"A nightmare, and you better wake up." I quickly explain what's happening.

She strains to wake up. I help her with a strong jolt, and she disappears.

As soon as I'm back in the tower of sleepers, I wake myself up.

Time to deal with the High Priest in the waking world.

CHAPTER THIRTY-FOUR

I LOOK up through my half-closed eyelids.

The High Priest clearly doesn't think me and Kit a threat. A lightning ball leaving his hands, he's focused on the stage, where Cadmael is approaching the bomb.

Puck. My nightmare is threatening to become reality.

Itzel's grandfather must remember what I told him about the threat of the other gnome. With surprising speed for his age, he turns and shoots a lightning ball into the path of the one flying at his head.

Boom.

Colliding just a few feet from the stage, the two lightning balls violently explode, the blast knocking Cadmael off his feet.

I glare at the High Priest.

Pucking bastard. He's ruined everything.

There are mere seconds left on the timer—no time for the older gnome to get up and disable the bomb.

Well, if I'm going to die, I'm going to hurt the one responsible before I go. Gritting my teeth at the pain, I raise my knife and stab the High Priest in the foot with all that remains of my strength.

He yells in pain and swings back his other foot to kick me—which is when Kit's giant fist smashes into his jaw.

The devastating punch causes the High Priest to fly up into the air, and as he lands, I make sure my knife is waiting for his heart.

His body jerks on top of me, a wheezing gasp exploding from his lips, and then he slumps, moving no more.

Kit rushes forward and yanks the bleeding gnome off my body.

For once, I'm not bothered by the bodily fluids on my skin.

Barely conscious, I glance at the stage.

Cadmael is on his feet again, but it's too late.

The countdown has reached zero.

Sucking in a breath, I brace for the explosion.

CHAPTER THIRTY-FIVE

THE BOMB KEEPS on beeping but doesn't explode.

I lock eyes with Kit, who looks as confused as I feel.

Then I recall my own question to Valerian: I wasn't sure if the countdown was to the explosion or to the moment the Icelus should leave to escape via the gates. Valerian thought it was the former, but it looks like the Icelus cult isn't suicidal.

The countdown was there to let them know when to bolt.

Which means we have time.

Some time. It's unclear how much.

Luckily, Cadmael isn't looking a gift centaur in the mouth. As soon as he realizes we're alive, he sprints over to the bomb and fiddles with it.

The longest minute of my life passes.

Twenty thousand gray hairs and a pint of my blood later, the reactor-bomb stops beeping. At the same exact moment, the elevator doors open, and a squadron of Senate Guard rushes into the room.

Weakly, I look up at Kit, who's turned into herself. "We're going to live?"

"Hush now." Kit crouches next to me and plants a soft kiss to my forehead. "All will be well."

Good, because I don't think I can hold on much longer.

Exhaling what I hope isn't my last breath, I pass out.

CHAPTER THIRTY-SIX

I COME TO.

Well, that's a relief. I half expected the afterlife, but I doubt this is it. I can hear familiar voices arguing in the distance—not something I'd expect after passing on.

I open my eyes. The hospital room is too bright, so I shut them again.

"Guys," Felix says. "I think she woke up."

I attempt Project Open Eyes once more. The faces of Ariel, Kit, Felix, Itzel, and Valerian are all within sneezing distance from my face, and all are speaking at the same time.

"You're okay." My voice is hoarse as I force out the words. "I was wor—"

"Here." Valerian grabs a glass of water from a table by my bed and places the straw sticking out of it into my mouth.

I take a small sip.

My throat feels better, and I realize I have an IV in

my arm, along with tubes in other places and monitoring equipment attached to my chest.

How bad was my condition for me to need all this?

"You're going to be fine," Valerian says as if reading my mind. "You had a nano surgery on your knee, and you should be able to walk on it, no problem. They didn't use any vampire blood during treatment, just pumped you with fluids. You lost so much blood you're bound to be weak."

"What about you?" I croak out, indeed feeling so weak the question takes an effort.

"All fine," he says, his sensual lips curved in a warm smile.

"The doctors here rely on vamp blood too much," Ariel grumbles. "I had to tell them repeatedly not to use it on me."

"Same," Felix says.

"I didn't need medical help." Kit winks at me. "Unlike some, I can handle myself in a fight."

Ariel and Felix object loudly, but I miss what they say due to a bout of dizziness. Breathing deeper, I crane my neck forward to catch the straw and suck in another sip. The cool water makes me feel a little better —until I accidentally spill some.

"You made her wet," Kit says to Valerian and pantomimes lasciviously with her eyebrows.

"Seriously?" Itzel asks at the same time as Ariel rolls her eyes and Felix slowly shakes his head.

"Did I hear you arguing earlier?" I ask, my voice finally my own. "You were loud."

Valerian gives everyone a narrow-eyed stare. "We don't want to worry her."

I feel all the blood drain from my face. "Is it Mom?"

Itzel shakes her head. "She's in the room next door, next to my grandfather."

Her grandfather, of course. I almost forgot. "Is he okay?" I ask.

"Fine, tell her," Valerian snaps. "All this guessing is worse."

"It's not Gramps," Itzel says. "Check any media feed. You'll understand."

I enable the VR and skim the headlines. "Oh. They know about the bomb."

Know is an understatement. The news outlets are reporting every tiny detail, and I soon learn why. Wrakar, the necromancer, scheduled a message to go out. In what they've dubbed the Necromancer Manifesto, he lamented that his kind were second-class citizens on Gomorrah and waxed poetic about how the bomb was justice for his people.

"What a pile of mooft crap." I turn off the VR. "Icelus didn't create the bomb for the necromancer kind. They did it to give people nightmares."

"Which they've succeeded in doing despite our efforts." Valerian's face looks so thunderous the others take a step back.

"I blame the Senate," Itzel says. "When the media asked them if the Necromancer Manifesto was true, they confirmed it, adding that they thwarted the plot."

Ariel curls her upper lip. "Typical politicians. Taking credit for our work."

Felix lifts his hand, as if to touch Valerian's tense shoulder, then decides against it. "Just give me the word, and I'll hack into—"

"No," Valerian says, noticeably calmer. "Icelus won this round. Messing with the media or the Senate would just make things worse."

I suck in another sip of water with a slurp. "They didn't win. Millions didn't die. We didn't die. True, this news will give some nightmares, but not nearly as many as would be the case if the bomb had actually gone off."

"Which is exactly what we were arguing about," Kit says. "Your boyfriend disagrees. He thinks the situation is worse now. The millions we saved are just more people to dream the nightmares."

Boyfriend? Is that what they all think?

Okay, I'll take it.

Valerian's jaw remains tight. He doesn't seem to have noticed Kit's premature labeling of our relationship—or if he does, he doesn't care. "What I'm saying is that Icelus succeeded," he says grimly.

"Only if you believe that nightmares really do feed some deity of theirs," I say. "But since all that is baloney, *we* won."

His stormy expression softens. "You're right," he says, though I don't think he means it. "More importantly, you need to rest."

Ah, that. He might be right there. The effort of

talking does make me feel like I've just completed a triathlon. Still, I'm not ready to get tucked in yet—not until I erase that worry from his gorgeous face.

"Can we talk in private?" I whisper, holding his gaze.

In an eyeblink, our surroundings change to a soothing meadow. My friends are no longer visible. Only Valerian is here, gazing down at me with those ocean-deep, hypnotic eyes.

"Can they hear us?" I ask.

He approaches the bed. "No. Can't see us either, at least not this version of us."

I try to sit up, but a wave of dizziness undercuts my efforts, so I settle for frowning up at him. "You almost died. Twice."

"We both did." His face twists with regret as he leans over me. "I'm sorry. I should've never gotten you involved."

"Then you'd be dead." If I had the energy to smack some sense into him, I would, but my arms feel too heavy at the moment.

"You don't understand," he says, frowning. "I—"

I push up onto my elbows and kiss him smack on the lips. His soft, yummy lips... My breathing quickens, a wave of heat chasing away the worst of the weakness as I—

An angry beep sounds, and Valerian abruptly pulls away. The illusion disappears, revealing the faces of my worried friends and the source of the noise—my heart monitor.

An uber nurse rushes into the room, moving almost too fast for my eyes to track. With the same speed, she examines me and adjusts the monitors before declaring that I'm fine but shouldn't be overstimulated in my current state.

I'm not sure I agree with that assessment. I'm not a doctor, but I feel like if Valerian stimulated me properly, I'd be good as new.

Unfortunately, that's not to be. The nurse herds everyone out of the room and goes to town on my IV, saying, "That should help you relax."

If by "relax" she means "go under," sure.

As my lids grow heavy, I realize something.

I kissed Valerian. In the real world. Without worrying about microbes.

That's huge. I can't wait until I'm all better, so I can make sure that wasn't just a fluke. There's going to be vigorous testing. Maybe double-blind control studies as well—as in, with both of us wearing blindfolds, and maybe handcuffs in his case.

With a smile on my face, I let the drug drag me under.

———

I WAKE UP FEELING BETTER. Infinitely better. The doctors must agree, as I only have some of the medical paraphernalia attached to me now.

Sitting up with ease, I look around.

The only other person in the room is Valerian. He's sleeping in a chair.

Aww. He stayed with me. That earns him another kiss. Maybe several.

My bladder yanks my mind from sexy thoughts to mundane reality.

I swing my legs down and see if I can stand up.

Yep. The knee is as good as new. I detach the heart monitor and the rest, and go into the bathroom to take care of business.

As I exit, I come face to face with Dr. Xipil.

"Ah, good. You're awake," he says.

I nod at the sleeping Valerian, then put a finger to my lips and gesture for the door. The gnome doctor nods, and we tiptoe out, closing the door behind us.

"I wanted to apologize," he says in a low voice. "I had no idea Dr. Cipactli was involved in a terrorist plot. Had I known—"

"Don't mention it." I beam a reassuring smile at him. "How's my mom?"

He glances at the nearby door. "We've just brought her back from the other hospital. Sadly, there's no change in her condition."

I walk over to the door in question and open it.

Seeing Mom hooked up to all those machines is again a punch to the heart—doubly painful now that I know she got this way because of me. I try not to dwell on that last part, though. Not when I can do something a lot more practical.

"I'd like to walk in her dreams again," I tell Dr. Xipil.

"Now?" He looks at the clock.

It's just past midnight.

I nod. "I'm feeling very strong. Can you get someone to help you subdue me in case I die during the subdream stage?"

He gestures in his VR, and a minute later, the uber nurse from before steps into the room.

We tell her what's what, and I approach Mom.

No touchless business now. I reach out and place my hand on her forehead.

"I'm sorry," I whisper. "I'll fix this."

Closing my eyes, I fall in.

CHAPTER THIRTY-SEVEN

A BLACK OCEAN is under my feet, and fiery skies are above my head. A huge creature is flying at me. It looks like an eyeball, but its eyelashes are snakes the size of anacondas—with fangs ready to bite.

A furry pitchfork grows out of my wrist.

The pupil of the giant eye dilates, and I get the strange feeling that a malevolent intelligence is examining me, scanning and filing away my every molecule.

The snake closest to me strikes at my neck. The fangs bite into my flesh, and I feel the poison beginning to spread through my bloodstream.

I thrust with my pitchfork.

The furry weapon enters the eyeball like a fork into jelly.

The snakes/eyelashes yelp in pain before slumping as one, creating the illusion of the eye closing.

———

I'M in my dream palace, blood gushing from the wound and my consciousness flickering in and out from the poison. I escape my body, heal the wound, and force the poison out, causing it to hang like a black cloud above me. Jumping back in, I dissipate the cloud and exhale a sigh of relief.

"Another close call." Pom's furry face is grim, his color black. "You need to stop doing this."

"I will as soon as Mom is out of her coma," I say and teleport to her nook in the tower of sleepers.

Making myself invisible, I touch Mom the same way as in the waking world.

———

A TEENAGE me is on the bathroom floor somewhere on Earth, if the primitive toilets are anything to go by. Her/my head is bashed in, brains spread out on the white tile. The windows in the place are black, so the only light comes from the flickering halogen lamps that add a macabre touch to the crime scene.

Mom stands above me holding a heavy porcelain toilet tank cover that's covered in blood.

Ugh. She couldn't bother to kill me in a more hygienic manner? I think I'd rather get my throat sliced with a scalpel—assuming it's sterile.

Ignoring Mom's nightmare, I gather all my power into a massive "wake up" jolt.

She doesn't wake up.

I close my eyes and strain so hard my nails pierce my palms.

This jolt doesn't work either.

Healing my wound, I try the jolt again. And again. And again.

After what feels like a thousand attempts, I have no choice but to give up.

The disappointment is bitter on my tongue. Only the knowledge that the *Lucid Dreamer* project isn't complete yet keeps me from utter despondency. I should get a much bigger boost when the game goes live, and I'll try it again then.

It's bound to work when I have more power. I have to believe that.

For now, I might as well jump out and let Mom be.

I'm about to do just that when my gaze lands on the black windows.

The secrets behind them call to me like sirens to lonely sailors.

Was Felix right? Is there something horrible Mom's hiding? Could she have tried to kill herself so I wouldn't learn whatever is behind one of these windows?

More importantly, could I use that secret to make her wake up?

Like the proverbial cat who bites the dust due to its overpowering curiosity, I float toward the nearest window.

Below me, Mom is too busy with her daughter slaughter to notice.

Before I can talk myself out of doing it, I fly into the onyx-like glass.

CHAPTER THIRTY-EIGHT

JUST LIKE BEFORE, I plunge into an icy black lake.

Previously, my powers couldn't help me swim to the shore, but what about now that I've gotten a boost?

I will myself to become lighter than water so I can float.

It doesn't help.

I will the water to become saltier, but that doesn't work either.

Fine. I'll swim.

Stroke after stroke, I edge closer to the nearest shore. I focus only on swimming. And swimming. And swimming. My breathing grows labored, yet the shore is still far away.

After what feels like hours, my every muscle starts to ache.

The shore is still a mile away.

I can't sink. If I do, I'll be kicked out of the dream world with my powers depleted. At least, that's what happened the last time I drowned under similar circumstances.

Desperately gulping in air, I swing my arms and kick with my legs, letting the motions become my only reality.

When a stray thought arises—like the one about the black windows I saw in Valerian's dreams—I banish it and refocus on the swim. When I'm about to give up, I meditate on a simple truth: My muscles are not really tearing into bits. It's not oxygen that I lack. This is just a dream.

This seems to help for a while, and eventually, I spot the shore nearby.

Harnessing all my willpower, I speed up so much Michael Phelps would be jealous.

As soon as my hand touches the dirt of the shore, the lake and the muscle spasms in my legs vanish without a trace.

———

MOM IS in a spacious room with three other people. There's a bathtub made of crystal in the middle, and she's floating in it.

Oh, and she's pregnant. More than pregnant—she's in the process of pushing the baby out.

Wow. Since this is a black-window memory, that means Mom doesn't remember giving birth to me. That must be odd.

Greedy for all the info, I examine the man holding

Mom's hand. He's got bronzed skin, amber eyes, and my chin.

My breath hitches.

Can it be?

"Push, honey." He kisses the back of Mom's hand. "That's it. I love you."

It has to be him. My father. The man I don't know anything about.

"Push!" the second person in the tub, the midwife, orders, staring intently at the crowning baby head.

Wait a second. The language they speak—I don't remember hearing it before, yet I understand perfectly.

"You're doing good," says an older woman holding Mom's other hand. "Almost there."

She looks just like Mom. A grandmother or an older sister, maybe—as in, my aunt?

The baby screams.

The midwife hands the gooey newborn to my father with a wide grin.

"It's a girl," he says, his eyes shining with joy. "A baby girl."

To my surprise, the midwife tells Mom, "Keep pushing."

Pushing after giving birth? Is it to get the placenta or something?

A second baby crowns.

Wait, what? I stare uncomprehendingly as the midwife goes through all the motions.

The second baby screams.

The midwife gives the second newborn to my mom.

What. Is. Happening?

"Do you know what you're going to call them?" the aunt/grandmother asks my father, taking the first infant from him.

He beams at her. "Asha, for my late mother." He looks at the baby in Mom's arms. "And Bailey, after her grandmother." He winks at the older woman—who must be the grandmother in question—and lifts the baby dubbed Bailey as if he were the monkey shaman presenting the new lion king.

My grandmother grins in delight and coos at the infants, but I don't register what she says.

My mind is spinning, my invisible mouth wide open.

A sister.

A twin.

Where is she? How come I don't remember anything about her? For that matter, where is my father? Or this namesake grandmother? Why don't I know anything about them either?

"Let me hold one," Mom says hoarsely, reaching for the baby-me when the memory transforms into another one.

———

MOM AND A MUCH OLDER ME—AROUND seven—are walking through the hub on Gomorrah.

Since the hub is on top of the skyscraper, there's a

great view down below, and both Mom and little me are staring at it as if they've never seen it before.

In fact, they look as though they've never seen a skyscraper before.

"This will be our new home," Mom says to little me, gesturing at the picturesque view.

"Our textile?" little me asks, eyes glued to the skyline.

"The word is *exile*. And we're never to speak of what happened before we came here."

Little me gives Mom a somber glance. "We're not?"

Mom crouches so our eyes are at the same level. "We've always lived here. Our lives before today were just a dream that we created using our powers."

The little me nods, her chin quivering.

I stare at them, stunned.

Could what Mom says be true?

Was the birth of two girls a memory of a dream?

No. My powers knew it was a real memory. Just as this one is.

"Let's go." Mom grabs little me by the hand, and the dream jumps to another memory.

———

WE'RE in a room covered from floor to ceiling with pottery paraphernalia, everything from wheel to kiln. Bailey, my grandmother, is molding a vase on the wheel. Looking on with a serene expression is Mom, who's holding two little girls by their hands.

Both resemble me, and I realize that my twin is of the identical variety—and that we were still together at this age, which must've been four or five.

That's definitely old enough to form memories, yet I don't recall this at all.

Oh, and it's clear that these memories are coming to me out of order: birth, seven, now four.

"Come, dear ones," the grandmother says.

The two little girls shuffle over.

"You can touch," she tells them.

Grinning mischievously, the twins leave palmprints on the sides of the vase.

The grandmother smiles in approval and deposits the vase into the kiln.

Wait a second.

I know that vase.

I broke it years later, on Gomorrah.

Mom was sad when it happened, as if it had sentimental value. Yet she couldn't have remembered this moment when the vase broke, not when the memory was locked in the black window.

Maybe these memories aren't as locked away as I thought—or the vase was precious simply as a memento from the forgotten past.

When the grandmother gives the vase to Mom as a gift, the memory terminates.

———

THIS ROOM IS the one where Asha and I were born.

Mom is holding my father's hand. Around them are a few adults I haven't seen before, though one man looks vaguely familiar. At their feet, my twin and I are about six years old and playing with two boys of similar ages. One of the boys also reminds me of someone, in the same indefinable way as the older man.

"I'm sorry, Davu. I don't think there's a choice," my father says to the familiar-looking man. "The prophecy—"

"Was vague," says Davu dismissively. "If—"

One of the boys pulls on his sleeve. "Dad, can Bailey and I go to the garden?"

Davu nods, and little me and the boy race out of the room.

"Mommy, can Kojo and I also go?" Asha asks.

Mom smiles. "Of course."

Giggling maniacally, my twin chases after the boy—Kojo—as if she were a werewolf and he a tasty hare.

As soon as they're out of the room, the memory terminates.

———

"WHERE'S BAILEY?" Asha asks Mom as they walk through alien-looking vegetation. Some of the enormous blue-green trees remind me of Earth's baobabs, others of sea coral.

"She's got an upset stomach," Mom says. "Daddy is with her."

With that, the memory ends, but another starts right away, a birthday party where my twin and I are playing with the boys from before, plus a dozen other children.

The next memory is of Mom tucking in the two twins, her face soft as she croons to us.

As I witness it all, I can't understand why Mom would want to forget all of this. Unless... is this black window something someone did to her? But if so, who? And why?

The common denominator in all these recollections seems to be Asha, my twin.

The next memory is of Mom, Dad, my sister, and me on a hike through a forest with that same alien vegetation. This time, I catch a glimpse of the sky—and exhale in wonder. Up above, besides clouds, are forests and buildings. The ground seems to warp upon itself, as if the planet we're on is not a sphere but an odd pretzel.

The next memory starts before I can puzzle out the strange geometry of the surroundings. It's of the four of us playing some game with cards made of an exotic material that reminds me of ivory.

Another memory follows, where Mom and the twins are watching the same strange sky at night. Not surprisingly, the star constellations are completely unfamiliar.

The peaceful stargazing shifts into yet another memory—and as I realize what I'm seeing, the pit of my stomach turns to ice.

CHAPTER THIRTY-NINE

MY SISTER and I look to be about seven. We're running through a clearing in the woods populated by the plants from the earlier memories.

Both girls are screaming in terror, and for a good reason.

Our parents are chasing after them with machetes made out of strange, non-shiny, ceramic-like material.

No. This can't be what it looks like. Surely the machetes are just for clearing vegetation, and this is some weird game. But the girls' terror seems all too real, and the weapons aside, something isn't right with our parents.

It's their faces. There's a magma-like fire in their eyes and a complete lack of emotion on their features.

Still, could this be a game regardless? Something to do with a holiday like Halloween?

A whole crowd of people is chasing after my

parents. In the front, I spot my grandmother, Davu with his wife and son, and Kojo and his parents.

"Stop!" Davu screams at my parents.

They don't respond, just keep chasing the girls.

One of the twins trips over a root.

The other keeps running for a few moments, then looks back, panting. "Asha, no!" my younger self gasps and rushes to her.

Asha is crying.

Little Bailey tries to lift her.

The parents close in.

Our father faces the crowd while Mom raises her machete.

"Mommy, no!" little me screams.

The machete whooshes by little Bailey's cheek and bites into Asha's neck.

Blood gushes out of the wound, spraying little me all over.

Asha's severed head rolls away.

Little Bailey screams.

I don't want to believe my eyes—except my eyes have nothing to do with what I've just witnessed, only my powers. And though I want to deny it, my powers leave no room for doubt.

This is a memory.

A memory that explains why I don't know my sister.

Numbly, I watch as Mom's strange eyes gaze at little me, who's sobbing uncontrollably. Then Mom's entire body tenses, her face twisting with alternating expressions of blankness and horror. Her eyes flicker between magma-like fire and normal brown, and her left hand grabs her right, as if trying to steal the machete from it. Finally, her eyes stay brown, and the horror eclipses all else on her face.

She looks at the bloody machete in her hands. Then at headless Asha.

With a raw, guttural moan, she spins around—just as my father smashes a fist into her temple.

The memory terminates.

———

THE NEXT MEMORY is of Mom reading a bedtime story to the three-year-old twins.

The one after that is another hike, but I barely pay attention to it.

I'm reeling, unable to process the impossible.

I had a sister, a twin, and Mom killed her.

That must be why she wanted to forget everything to do with Asha, and why she was so terrified to have me dreamwalk in her. Some part of her must know that she forgot something awful—and this might even explain the dreams where she was killing me. I look just like Asha would if she were alive.

Those nightmares echoed the terrible truth.

Mom killed my sister.

No wonder she's been depressed for as long as I've known her. Even without recalling the details, she must've been in constant psychic pain.

And is this why I don't remember Asha either? Because I witnessed her murder at the hand of our mother? I'm no shrink, but children have been known to block out traumas far less significant than this.

Why did Mom do this? And what was the deal with her eyes at the time of the murder? That magma I saw in her gaze was weirdly familiar. It's almost like—

The memories halt, and I find myself in an environment that reminds me of those eyes.

Black ocean is under my feet, with skies that seem to be on fire up above.

It's the place where subdream monsters attack, only I'm not in a subdream.

In fact, I've only seen this backdrop outside of subdreams once—when I dreamwalked in that necromancer.

Puck. I completely forgot about that until now.

A presence congeals out of nothingness to stand on the ocean in front of me, a humanoid creature of enormous proportions.

It's a frightening sight, even if it's hard to pinpoint why. The face looking at me is just as beautiful as the last time, with features that have a supernatural kind of symmetry.

It's the exact same face as in the necromancer's dream, though logic states he and my mom shouldn't be dreaming the same thing.

Not unless they both somehow saw it.

The black holes on the terribly beautiful face scan

me more carefully this time, and all I can do is stand there and stare up at it, paralyzed.

"You're you. And alive." Like in the necromancer's dream, its booming voice conjures my every fear.

I swallow hard. "Who are you? What are you?"

"I'm Phobetor." The vibrations of the being's reply make the blood freeze in my veins, even before I comprehend the significance of that name. "Your existence is a blight."

My stunned mind latches on to the strange phrase. A blight—that's what the subdream monsters said to me earlier. This must be the master they were talking about, not Mom.

Phobetor's black-hole eyes narrow, and its truck-sized arm reaches for me.

With an impossible effort of will, I snap out of my paralysis and jolt myself awake.

———

BACK IN THE REAL WORLD, I hold myself together long enough to reassure the uber nurse and Dr. Xipil that I'm not homicidally insane. Then I rush into the bathroom and empty my stomach.

When I can breathe again, I let myself process the last thing I saw.

The terrible, beautiful being called itself Phobetor— same as the deity Icelus worship. A god of nightmares, said to benefit from all the misfortune in the Cogniverse.

It's impossible.

Unthinkable.

Utterly ridiculous.

I can't believe I'm even entertaining this idea, but... are Icelus right?

Does Phobetor really exist?

If so, what does he have to do with me and my mom?

I stare at my ashen face in the mirror, the damning memory-dream I just witnessed playing in front of my eyes. Asha and me, our parents with machetes... the strange hue of their eyes...

And Phobetor, right there in Mom's dreams.

A million questions race through my mind, but I can only latch on to one.

If Phobetor is real, is he the reason for the horror I witnessed?

Is he why Mom killed my twin?

SNEAK PEEKS

Thank you for reading! I hope you're loving Bailey's story! Her adventures continue in *Dream Chaser (The Bailey Spade Series: Book 3).*

The god of nightmares is real? How fun.

A mystery dreamwalker is trying to turn me homicidally insane? Business as usual.

But when a legendary seer gets involved, we end up on a world populated by necromancers. Oops. I'll have to put on my big dreamwalker panties and learn to forgive Valerian's betrayal before we're all killed by Icelus... or zombies... or a deadly virus.

Visit my website at www.dimazales.com to get your copy today!

Do you want to be notified of my new releases? Sign up for my email list at www.dimazales.com!

Love audiobooks? This series, and all of my other books, are available in audio.

Want to read my other books? You can check out:

- *The Sasha Urban Series* - the fantastical urban fantasy series set in the same universe as Bailey Spade, where Felix and Ariel first appear
- *Mind Dimensions* - the action-packed urban fantasy adventures of Darren, who can stop time and read minds
- *Upgrade* - the thrilling sci-fi tale of Mike Cohen, whose new technology will transform our brains *and* the world
- *The Last Humans* - the futuristic sci-fi/dystopian story of Theo, who lives in a world where nothing is as it seems
- *The Sorcery Code* - the epic fantasy adventures of sorcerer Blaise and his creation, the beautiful and powerful Gala

And now, please turn the page for a sneak peek at Chapter 1 of *Dream Chaser* and an excerpt from *The Thought Readers* (*Mind Dimensions: Book 1*).

SNEAK PEEK AT DREAM CHASER

I stumble out of the bathroom in Mom's hospital room and nearly collide with Dr. Xipil.

"Are you okay?" the gnome doctor asks.

I'm far from okay, but if I tell him why, he might want to have me talk to a shrink. The injuries I suffered during the fight with Icelus are healed, but mentally and emotionally, I'm a wreck.

Case in point: I'm seriously considering the existence of Phobetor, the god of nightmares Icelus worship. Worse yet, I'm wondering if said deity made my mom kill my sister.

What little blood had returned to my face rushes away again.

I had a sister. A twin.

It's as hard to wrap my mind around that fact as it is to fathom my mom killing her.

Her name was Asha, and I watched her die before I'd even accepted the fact that she'd existed.

What I wouldn't give for a chance to have met her, or to at least remember her.

"Do you want to lie down?" Dr. Xipil asks, sounding more worried. "You look like you're about to pass out."

I give him a forced smile. "I'm fine. Just disappointed I failed to rouse Mom."

Dr. Xipil glances at the bed where Mom lies and sighs. "You'll try again. You're bound to succeed eventually."

Not ready to discuss an evil deity that might be waiting for me in Mom's dreams, I simply nod.

Mom looks serene in her comatose state. Calm, even. But that has to be a lie. Her dreams are of killing a daughter—because that's what she'd done in the waking world.

In a very real way, I don't know my own mother. Makes me wonder if you can know anyone, or trust them.

The doctor clears his throat. "You have loyal friends."

Puck. I have to snap out of this, or the good doctor will insist I go back to my hospital bed.

I head for the door, and as casually as I can, ask, "What makes you say that?"

"They all recovered much faster than you did, but they wouldn't leave your side until your husband chased them away." He opens the door for me.

"My husband?" I'm too shocked to walk through.

Dr. Xipil gestures at my room across the hall. "Boyfriend?"

"Oh, you mean Valerian." I step out into the hallway. "He's neither my husband nor my boyfriend."

Not yet—but fingers crossed.

The corners of Dr. Xipil's eyes crinkle. "Are you sure he knows that? Because he definitely acted like a significant other while you were under. The nursing staff and I had to walk on eggshells."

Really? Aww. "Sounds like I should check on him."

"Good idea. If he wakes up and you're not there, he'll freak."

"Oh, come on, that doesn't sound like him."

"You didn't see what I saw," the doctor says. "If you need anything else, let me know tomorrow afternoon. My shift is now officially over."

I thank him, and he hurries away as I head over to my room.

Sticking my head in, I see Valerian slumped in a chair, his dark, thick hair disheveled around his beautifully symmetrical face. His intense ocean-blue eyes are closed, his kissable lips slightly parted.

Quietly, I tiptoe in. He's in REM sleep, according to my newfound REM-sensing ability and the fact that his eyes are moving behind his eyelids.

Hmm. Maybe I don't need to wake him. The fact that he's dreaming is an opportunity. I could, for example, talk to him in his sleep... or snoop in those black windows he's got.

Yep. I'm going for it.

Resisting the temptation to walk over and touch his

chiseled face, I initiate the dreamwalk remotely. Might as well practice the new power.

Just as I did with Itzel's grandfather, I imagine standing next to Valerian, close enough to breathe in his clean pine scent. I imagine touching his carved jaw and picture how that hint of stubble would feel under my fingers. I imagine how my heart would beat faster and heat would spread—

To my disappointment, I don't need to imagine this further, because with the familiar whiff of ozone and the sensation of falling, I drop into his dream.

———

As soon as I appear in the surreally colored, manna-scented lobby of my dream palace, Pom shows up—and between the expression on the looft's furry face and his deep black coloring, I can tell he knows a lot of what I've learned in Mom's black window.

Taking the scenic route to the tower of sleepers, I fill in any details Pom doesn't know and reassure him that I don't magically have the answers to his million questions—and that I'd like to know the why and how of Phobetor and my twin as much as he does.

"Ah," Pom says sagely when he spots Valerian sleeping on his bed. "You're here looking for a distraction."

I brush my fingers over Valerian's dimpled chin without willing myself to go in yet. "I guess you could say that."

Pom's triangular ears take on a light orange hue. "And how are things going between the two of you?"

"What?"

The pupils in his lavender eyes morph into red hearts. "Are you in love?"

I jerk my hand away from Valerian's face. "Are you crazy? I don't even know what that would feel like. We barely know each other. Plus—"

"You might be overthinking it." Pom perches on my shoulder. "Is it because you've never had a boyfriend?"

I shoo him off. "I'm thinking just the right amount. You should give that a try someday."

He lands on the edge of Valerian's bed. "Just don't go looking for reasons not to love him. We both know you want to."

It's official. I'm getting love-life advice from a looft, a creature that reproduces by asexual budding.

Shaking my head, I dive into Valerian's dream.

———

Visit www.dimazales.com to learn more!

SNEAK PEEK AT THE THOUGHT READERS

Description

Everyone thinks I'm a genius.

Everyone is wrong.

Sure, I finished Harvard at eighteen and now make crazy money at a hedge fund. But that's not because I'm unusually smart or hard-working.

It's because I cheat.

You see, I have a unique ability. I can go outside time into my own personal version of reality—the place I call "the Quiet"—where I can explore my surroundings while the rest of the world stands still.

I thought I was the only one who could do this—until I met *her*.

My name is Darren, and this is how I learned that I'm a Reader.

Excerpt

Sometimes I think I'm crazy. I'm sitting at a casino table in Atlantic City, and everyone around me is motionless. I call this the *Quiet*, as though giving it a name makes it seem more real—as though giving it a name changes the fact that all the players around me are frozen like statues, and I'm walking among them, looking at the cards they've been dealt.

The problem with the theory of my being crazy is that when I 'unfreeze' the world, as I just have, the cards the players turn over are the same ones I just saw in the Quiet. If I were crazy, wouldn't these cards be different? Unless I'm so far gone that I'm imagining the cards on the table, too.

But then I also win. If that's a delusion—if the pile of chips on my side of the table is a delusion—then I might as well question everything. Maybe my name isn't even Darren.

No. I can't think that way. If I'm really that confused, I don't want to snap out of it—because if I do, I'll probably wake up in a mental hospital.

Besides, I love my life, crazy and all.

My shrink thinks the Quiet is an inventive way I

describe the 'inner workings of my genius.' Now that sounds crazy to me. She also might want me, but that's beside the point. Suffice it to say, she's as far as it gets from my datable age range, which is currently right around twenty-four. Still young, still hot, but done with school and pretty much beyond the clubbing phase. I hate clubbing, almost as much as I hated studying. In any case, my shrink's explanation doesn't work, as it doesn't account for the way I know things even a genius wouldn't know—like the exact value and suit of the other players' cards.

I watch as the dealer begins a new round. Besides me, there are three players at the table: Grandma, the Cowboy, and the Professional, as I call them. I feel that now almost imperceptible fear that accompanies the phasing. That's what I call the process: phasing into the Quiet. Worrying about my sanity has always facilitated phasing; fear seems helpful in this process.

I phase in, and everything gets quiet. Hence the name for this state.

It's eerie to me, even now. Outside the Quiet, this casino is very loud: drunk people talking, slot machines, ringing of wins, music—the only place louder is a club or a concert. And yet, right at this moment, I could probably hear a pin drop. It's like I've gone deaf to the chaos that surrounds me.

Having so many frozen people around adds to the strangeness of it all. Here is a waitress stopped mid-step, carrying a tray with drinks. There is a woman about to pull a slot machine lever. At my own table, the dealer's hand is raised, the last card he dealt hanging unnaturally in midair. I walk up to him from the side of the table and reach for it. It's a king, meant for the Professional. Once I let the card go, it falls on the table rather than continuing to float as before—but I know full well that it will be back in the air, in the exact position it was when I grabbed it, when I phase out.

The Professional looks like someone who makes money playing poker, or at least the way I always imagined someone like that might look. Scruffy, shades on, a little sketchy-looking. He's been doing an excellent job with the poker face—basically not twitching a single muscle throughout the game. His face is so expressionless that I wonder if he might've gotten Botox to help maintain such a stony countenance. His hand is on the table, protectively covering the cards dealt to him.

I move his limp hand away. It feels normal. Well, in a manner of speaking. The hand is sweaty and hairy, so moving it aside is unpleasant and is admittedly an abnormal thing to do. The normal part is that the hand is warm, rather than cold. When I was a kid, I expected people to feel cold in the Quiet, like stone statues.

With the Professional's hand moved away, I pick up his cards. Combined with the king that was hanging in the air, he has a nice high pair. Good to know.

I walk over to Grandma. She's already holding her cards, and she has fanned them nicely for me. I'm able to avoid touching her wrinkled, spotted hands. This is a relief, as I've recently become conflicted about touching people—or, more specifically, women—in the Quiet. If I had to, I would rationalize touching Grandma's hand as harmless, or at least not creepy, but it's better to avoid it if possible.

In any case, she has a low pair. I feel bad for her. She's been losing a lot tonight. Her chips are dwindling. Her losses are due, at least partially, to the fact that she has a terrible poker face. Even before looking at her cards, I knew they wouldn't be good because I could tell she was disappointed as soon as her hand was dealt. I also caught a gleeful gleam in her eyes a few rounds ago when she had a winning three of a kind.

This whole game of poker is, to a large degree, an exercise in reading people—something I really want to get better at. At my job, I've been told I'm great at reading people. I'm not, though; I'm just good at using the Quiet to make it seem like I am. I do want to learn how to read people for real, though. It would be nice to know what everyone is thinking.

What I don't care that much about in this poker game is money. I do well enough financially to not have to depend on hitting it big gambling. I don't care if I win or lose, though quintupling my money back at the blackjack table was fun. This whole trip has been more about going gambling because I finally can, being twenty-one and all. I was never into fake IDs, so this is an actual milestone for me.

Leaving Grandma alone, I move on to the next player—the Cowboy. I can't resist taking off his straw hat and trying it on. I wonder if it's possible for me to get lice this way. Since I've never been able to bring back any inanimate objects from the Quiet, nor otherwise affect the real world in any lasting way, I figure I won't be able to get any living critters to come back with me, either.

Dropping the hat, I look at his cards. He has a pair of aces—a better hand than the Professional. Maybe the Cowboy is a professional, too. He has a good poker face, as far as I can tell. It'll be interesting to watch those two in this round.

Next, I walk up to the deck and look at the top cards, memorizing them. I'm not leaving anything to chance.

When my task in the Quiet is complete, I walk back to myself. Oh, yes, did I mention that I see myself sitting there, frozen like the rest of them? That's the weirdest part. It's like having an out-of-body experience.

Approaching my frozen self, I look at him. I usually avoid doing this, as it's too unsettling. No amount of looking in the mirror—or seeing videos of yourself on YouTube—can prepare you for viewing your own three-dimensional body up close. It's not something anyone is meant to experience. Well, aside from identical twins, I guess.

It's hard to believe that this person is me. He looks more like some random guy. Well, maybe a bit better than that. I do find this guy interesting. He looks cool. He looks smart. I think women would probably consider him good-looking, though I know that's not a modest thing to think.

It's not like I'm an expert at gauging how attractive a guy is, but some things are common sense. I can tell when a dude is ugly, and this frozen me is not. I also know that generally, being good-looking requires a symmetrical face, and the statue of me has that. A strong jaw doesn't hurt, either. Check. Having broad shoulders is a positive, and being tall really helps. All covered. I have blue eyes—that seems to be a plus. Girls have told me they like my eyes, though right now, on the frozen me, the eyes look creepy—glassy. They look like the eyes of a lifeless wax figure.

Realizing that I'm dwelling on this subject way too long, I shake my head. I can just picture my shrink analyzing this moment. Who would imagine admiring themselves like this as part of their mental illness? I can just picture her scribbling down *Narcissist*, underlining it for emphasis.

Enough. I need to leave the Quiet. Raising my hand, I touch my frozen self on the forehead, and I hear noise again as I phase out.

Everything is back to normal.

The card that I looked at a moment before—the king that I left on the table—is in the air again, and from there it follows the trajectory it was always meant to, landing near the Professional's hands. Grandma is still eyeing her fanned cards in disappointment, and the Cowboy has his hat on again, though I took it off him in the Quiet. Everything is exactly as it was.

On some level, my brain never ceases to be surprised at the discontinuity of the experience in the Quiet and outside it. As humans, we're hardwired to question reality when such things happen. When I was trying to outwit my shrink early on in my therapy, I once read an entire psychology textbook during our session. She, of course, didn't notice it, as I did it in the Quiet. The book talked about how babies as young as two months old are surprised if they see something out of the ordinary, like gravity appearing to work backwards. It's no wonder my brain has trouble adapting. Until I was ten, the world behaved normally, but everything has been weird since then, to put it mildly.

Glancing down, I realize I'm holding three of a kind. Next time, I'll look at my cards before phasing. If I have something this strong, I might take my chances and play fair.

The game unfolds predictably because I know everybody's cards. At the end, Grandma gets up. She's clearly lost enough money.

And that's when I see the girl for the first time.

She's hot. My friend Bert at work claims that I have a 'type,' but I reject that idea. I don't like to think of myself as shallow or predictable. But I might actually be a bit of both, because this girl fits Bert's description of my type to a T. And my reaction is extreme interest, to say the least.

Large blue eyes. Well-defined cheekbones on a slender face, with a hint of something exotic. Long, shapely legs, like those of a dancer. Dark wavy hair in a ponytail—a hairstyle that I like. And without bangs—even better. I hate bangs—not sure why girls do that to themselves. Though lack of bangs is not, strictly speaking, in Bert's description of my type, it probably should be.

I continue staring at her. With her high heels and tight skirt, she's overdressed for this place. Or maybe I'm underdressed in my jeans and t-shirt. Either way, I don't care. I have to try to talk to her.

I debate phasing into the Quiet and approaching her, so I can do something creepy like stare at her up close, or maybe even snoop in her pockets. Anything to help me when I talk to her.

I decide against it, which is probably the first time that's ever happened.

I know that my reasoning for breaking my usual habit—if you can even call it that—is strange. I picture the following chain of events: she agrees to date me, we go out for a while, we get serious, and because of the deep connection we have, I come clean about the Quiet. She learns I did something creepy and has a fit, then dumps me. It's ridiculous to think this, of course, considering that we haven't even spoken yet. Talk about jumping the gun. She might have an IQ below seventy, or the personality of a piece of wood. There can be twenty different reasons why I wouldn't want to date her. And besides, it's not all up to me. She might tell me to go fuck myself as soon as I try to talk to her.

Still, working at a hedge fund has taught me to

hedge. As crazy as that reasoning is, I stick with my decision not to phase because I know it's the gentlemanly thing to do. In keeping with this unusually chivalrous me, I also decide not to cheat at this round of poker.

As the cards are dealt again, I reflect on how good it feels to have done the honorable thing—even without anyone knowing. Maybe I should try to respect people's privacy more often. As soon as I think this, I mentally snort. *Yeah, right.* I have to be realistic. I wouldn't be where I am today if I'd followed that advice. In fact, if I made a habit of respecting people's privacy, I would lose my job within days—and with it, a lot of the comforts I've become accustomed to.

Copying the Professional's move, I cover my cards with my hand as soon as I receive them. I'm about to sneak a peek at what I was dealt when something unusual happens.

The world goes quiet, just like it does when I phase in... but I did nothing this time.

And at that moment, I see *her*—the girl sitting across the table from me, the girl I was just thinking about. She's standing next to me, pulling her hand away from mine. Or, strictly speaking, from my frozen self's hand—as I'm standing a little to the side looking at her.

She's also still sitting in front of me at the table, a frozen statue like all the others.

My mind goes into overdrive as my heartbeat jumps. I don't even consider the possibility of that second girl being a twin sister or something like that. I know it's her. She's doing what I did just a few minutes ago. She's walking in the Quiet. The world around us is frozen, but we are not.

A horrified look crosses her face as she realizes the same thing. Before I can react, she lunges across the table and touches her own forehead.

The world becomes normal again.

She stares at me from across the table, shocked, her eyes huge and her face pale. Her hands tremble as she rises to her feet. Without so much as a word, she turns and begins walking away, then breaks into a run a couple of seconds later.

Getting over my own shock, I get up and run after her. It's not exactly smooth. If she notices a guy she doesn't know running after her, dating will be the last thing on her mind. But I'm beyond that now. She's the only person I've met who can do what I do. She's proof that I'm not insane. She might have what I want most in the world.

She might have answers.

Visit www.dimazales.com to learn more!

ABOUT THE AUTHOR

Dima Zales is a *New York Times* and *USA Today* bestselling author of science fiction and fantasy. Prior to becoming a writer, he worked in the software development industry in New York as both a programmer and an executive. From high-frequency trading software for big banks to mobile apps for popular magazines, Dima has done it all. In 2013, he left the software industry in order to concentrate on his writing career and moved to Palm Coast, Florida, where he currently resides.

Please visit www.dimazales.com to learn more.